ABOUT THE
DARK HART COLLECTION

THE DARK HART COLLECTION is a line of novels and novellas curated by me, Sadie Hartmann, aka "Mother Horror," for Dark Matter INK. These stories map new territories in the ever-evolving landscape of the horror genre. I invite you to escape into books written by authors who blur the lines between multiple genres, and who explore the depth and breadth of dark hearts everywhere.

Sincerely,

Sadie Hartmann
Curator, The Dark Hart Collection

PRAISE FOR
I CAN SEE YOUR LIES

"Intimate, twisty, and compelling. *I Can See Your Lies* is an excellent showcase for the horror writer-director's prose storytelling chops. Izzy Lee is here to stay."

—Christopher Golden, *New York Times* bestselling author of *Road of Bones* and *All Hallows*

"Arresting, cinematic, smart. A mist advances across this book, born of its warmth and frost. The freaky past informs the present, just as the unnerving present unearths the past. Hollywood opprobrium, familial enigmas, twists and turns and truth. Steel yourself: Izzy Lee will thrill you apart."

—Josh Malerman, *New York Times* bestselling author of *Bird Box* and *Incidents Around the House*

"Fast. Sharp. Mysterious. Haunting. Nightmarish. This is one hell of a debut from a very talented storyteller, with a cinematic eye. Lee delivers."

—Gabino Iglesias, author of Shirley Jackson and Bram Stoker award-winning novel, *The Devil Takes you Home*

"Izzy Lee offers us all front-row seats to a particularly haunted Hollywood, where celluloid ghosts forever walk down the red carpet of their own blood and former glory."

—Clay McLeod Chapman, author of *Ghost Eaters* and
The Remaking

"Fearless writing meets electric, imaginative storytelling in Izzy Lee's *I Can See Your Lies.* This short, chilling novella establishes Lee as an exciting and vital voice in contemporary horror fiction."

—Eric LaRocca, *New York Times* bestselling author of
Things Have Gotten Worse Since We Last Spoke

"*I Can See Your Lies* is as captivating as it is unsettling. A cerebral supernatural thriller starring the glittering darkness of Hollywood. Izzy Lee will make you question what is past and what is present."

—Cynthia Pelayo, Bram Stoker Award winning author
of *Crime Scene*

"Fiercely imaginative, dripping with Hollywood ooze, this is a biting tale about lies, weaponized deceit, and a woman's role in both the home and the heart, where Tinseltown is as sordid as the visions Fin sees on the faces of those around her. Assured and moving. Lee is one to watch."

—Gemma Amor, Bram Stoker and British Fantasy Award
nominated author of *Full Immersion* and *Dear Laura*

"*I Can See Your Lies* is wonderful fun, a spooky good debut from an author on their way up. The sky is the limit for Izzy Lee."

—C. S. Humble, author of *The Light of a Black Star*

"A Lynchian horror-thriller that boils hot just before an explosive third act, and it might be my favorite read of the year. *I Can See Your Lies* will leave your brain scattered."

—Tim Meyer, author of *The Switch House* and *Malignant Summer*

"An unsettling and unpredictable novella, *I Can See Your Lies* mixes the paranormal with the trauma of family history and the darkness of Hollywood. Lee's story of a complicated female protagonist will take more twists than you'll ever see coming. A must-read for die-hard horror fans, this book will leave you wondering about humanity's hidden darkness."

—Brea Grant, director of *Torn Hearts* and *12 Hour Shift*

"Izzy Lee's novella, *I Can See Your Lies,* is a fantastic debut! Lee showcases her signature furiosity while also demonstrating she can sustain both her passion and our captivation over a farther-reaching tale. Like her film work, the only thing *I Can See Your Lies* leave me wanting is more Izzy Lee!"

—Bracken MacLeod, Shirley Jackson Award nominated author of *Closing Costs* and *13 Views of the Suicide Woods*

"Izzy Lee has swiftly established herself as a powerful and progressive voice in film, and now turns her blazing bright eye for story to the page. Her debut novella grabs the reader from the first page, pulling them into a tale of self-discovery and multi-generational trauma. With flavors of true crime and the supernatural woven within, *I Can See Your Lies* is a genre-bending blast that's sure to please."

—Laurel Hightower, author of *Crossroads* and *Below*

"Acclaimed filmmaker Izzy Lee brings her prodigious storytelling skills to the page with her debut novella, *I Can See Your Lies,* an incisive, supernatural tale of inherited trauma and everyday aggressions."

—Joshua Chaplinsky, author of *Letters to the Purple Satin Killer* and *Kanye West—Reanimator*

"A beautifully blended deep dive of supernatural noir, where you suspect everyone and you're still wrong. *I Can See Your Lies* examines old-Hollywood behaviors with new standards, and races toward the twisted outcome."

—Kelli Owen, author of *The Headless Boy* and the *Wilted Lilies* series

"I can see it on your face. You're going to love this book. *I Can See Your Lies* delves into a power none of us truly wish to possess. When you can see the truth, everything changes, even the pieces you didn't think would be affected. Izzy Lee explores this horror, alongside family relationships, guilt, trauma, and grief. A fast-paced ride straight into hell, *I Can See Your Lies* will lead you to the truth and leave you questioning everything you thought you knew. Highly recommended."

—James Sabata, author of *Caduceus*

"Award-winning filmmaker Izzy Lee has written her first horror novella, and boy, what an extraordinary and vivid tale it is. *I Can See Your Lies* is an engrossing, ingenious, and gripping story that I devoured in one sitting. If you love ghost stories, tales of revenge, and the gradual reveal of family secrets, coupled with possession of a supernatural power that can certainly be a poisoned chalice at times, then this one is for you. Highly recommended."

—Barbie Wilde, actress (*Hellbound: Hellraiser II; Death Wish 3*) and author of *The Venus Complex, Voices of the Damned*

I CAN

SEE

YOUR

LIES

CONTENT WARNINGS

Murder, Violence, Domestic Abuse

Reader discretion is advised.

Edited by Rob Carroll
Book Design and Layout by Rob Carroll
Cover Art and Design by Olly Jeavons

ISBN 978-1-958598-28-3 (paperback)
ISBN 978-1-958598-63-4 (eBook)

darkmatter-ink.com

I CAN SEE YOUR LIES

A NOVELLA BY IZZY LEE

DARK
MATTER
INK

For Steve, my cosmic love. For all time. Always.

ACT 1:
LOS ANGELES

SATURDAY

THE SCARLET POOL expanded over the rug, widening, consuming. The cream-colored shag carpet drank up the red liquid in a furious fit of greed, and Fin's horror and the ratcheting anxiety that screeched within her cells never abated. The feelings were as intense as the first time she saw the puddle of blood.

No, she corrected herself. She was more terrified than ever.

I've never seen the vision while awake.

Today, that changed. Her somewhat ordinary nightmare (*if that was a thing*) broke through into her waking life, transforming her plate of rotini and sauce into a breathtaking cause for alarm. Lunch had transformed itself into blood and carpet.

Fin swallowed, staring up at the table from where she had toppled off her chair.

Was it still there? Could she trust herself? She slowly crawled back onto her haunches until the edge of the plate appeared, towering over her on the high-top table.

It's only lunch, you silly bitch, came the words in her head, and immediately cringed at the harsh voice. But if it were only lunch, why was she so freaked out? Fin shivered. The fact was, she knew damn well that the food in question was much more than a typical meal.

The same image had flashed in her dreams for years. It wasn't every night, or even every week, but Fin saw it more than enough, beginning when she turned the vulnerable age of thirteen. Maybe her mind finally had enough of the strange vision, which was altogether quite different and far scarier than the bubbles. Maybe she'd fractured. She could call someone. She *should* call someone. But what would they do with her? They'd lock her up, put her on a regimen of medication so heavy-duty that she'd never see the vision again.

At this point, that'd be just fine. If only the rest of Fin's mind didn't go on a vacation as well. The drugs would blot out all agency and most of her consciousness. Besides, there was no guarantee that the visions would actually stop. She knew how these things worked. She'd been on these kinds of drugs before—as a teenager at the mercy of an aunt who'd meant well, a father who didn't, and clueless medical professionals. Those who'd prescribe anything they considered helpful or whatever new drug the pharmaceutical companies pushed.

The pills came in benign shapes and happy pastel colors, but none of them helped. All this for telling the truth about what she saw—mostly for those damned black bubbles appearing on the face of anyone who lied to her. Sometimes, like now, the visions were far more horrifying. As a consequence for speaking up—*for the mere crime of asking for help*—she got help, but it wasn't the kind of help she needed or wanted. Months of her life had fallen into the void, and she was in no way eager to return to that particular trauma. *Non-trauma?* A bad hand she'd been dealt? What was trauma anyway, in this case?

Her mind skipped back in time to her father. The image of his handsome, cold face, when he decided to surrender her to the mental hospital, was one she'd never forget—*like this puddle of blood.* Worse, he had someone else deliver her to the ward. He even had the gall to say out loud that he was a high-profile actor and *couldn't be seen doing that*, so he'd ordered his beleaguered personal assistant to do it. Aided by two hulking security guards, the three of them, these virtual strangers, had handed her over to Hell.

Beyond the monotonous, eggshell-hued walls, she recalled the echoes of her screams and struggles—but not much else. As hard as she tried, the holes in her memory allowed her to see no further into her imprisonment. No, she hadn't been in jail, but she'd been forcibly put away against her will. Drugged. Locked and filed away for social adjustment. *Postponed.*

She couldn't help but wonder if anyone, an orderly or doctor, had taken advantage of her while she'd been in that kind of state. Unfortunately, this kind of atrocity had been committed against women far too often. It was less common in modern times, but she was smart enough to know that villains gravitated towards professions where they could prey on the vulnerable. *Hell, I've lived it.* Her body would remember, even if her mind built a fortress from knowing such harsh truths. She might never know if she was violated and how many times, and that right there was a pretty good reason to never let anyone tinker with her brain again. A chill washed over her, cooling her flesh and dotting it with goosebumps.

Like many, many women who had come before her (*too many, most of us*), Fin had learned that speaking truth to power (*or speaking about anything deemed unpleasant at all*) often resulted in punishment. Whether that meant derision, outright abuse, or getting locked away until she learned better, it all really meant one thing: *shut up*. Be silent, be quiet, do not disturb us, go away, we don't want to deal with your inconvenient experience. We have no need for it, just shut the hell up and look pretty, *serve* us, that's the only thing you're good at in our minds, and if you challenge us, you're going to fucking regret it, *girl*.

After that ordeal, Fin never let herself forget that she lived in a world not made for her at all, but one specifically designed to keep her in her place.

When you finally see society for what it is, for what it does to people who are not the controlling party, you see inequality everywhere. You cannot unsee it, or wipe it from memory. The system works exactly as intended. Even though it's exactly what they want, staying quiet becomes a survival mechanism. There's no way to win.

Focus.

Fin took a breath and forced these truths out of her head in order to deal with the current, terrifying concern at hand.

She closed her eyes and inhaled deep enough to reach her core, her muscles expanding and stretching to let in relief. *Inhale for 1, 2, 3, 4… And exhale out for 1, 2, 3, 4…* She repeated the process, recalling her anti-anxiety techniques until she was able to push herself off the floor. Slow, steady, she rose to her full height, her gaze still on the carpet. The blood was gone.

There *was*, however, a large spot on the carpet, and it looked as though someone had recently attempted to scrub the spot clean.

Huh.

Fin bent down and touched the spot where the rug fibers were compressed. Still damp. She rubbed two fingers together and sniffed—a faint, chemical odor of enzyme carpet cleaner lingered on her skin. *Odd.* She couldn't recall cleaning the rug. It was doubtful that Jeff would have cleaned up a mess, unless he'd been desperate to get rid of something and she wasn't around to do it for him—as his dutiful wife and servant. It was entirely possible that she dissociated while tidying up. It had happened before. But she also had a vivid recollection of the stir-fry dinner that wound up on the floor.

When Jeff went on a tirade, her mind and voice tended to go quiet. De-escalation usually worked, but there were times when Fin's silence upset her husband even more. When he wanted to get a reaction out of her, he became even louder and more violent. It was like an ember erupting into flames. Except that it wasn't. *No, it was like watching a toddler in the body of a full-grown man throw a tantrum.*

She wondered how far things could escalate.

Her pulse quickened again. Fin drew in another long breath of air to ground herself, but breathing with mindful intention would only go so far today—she'd need another alternative. She looked to her feet, focused on the fuzzy house socks she wore: soft stripes in blue and violet and cream. One stripe, two stripes, three stripes, four… A few more long breaths, and she could function.

If I can piece together the recent past, my present will become clear.

Fin closed her eyes and thought back to the chaos of the last few days.

THURSDAY

A RAY OF sunlight reflected off the windshield of a passing car and into Fin's eyes. She squinted and watched the school bus drive away, her daughter Marnie aboard.

"I'll be going out after work with a couple of the guys," Jeff said.

She looked to the man she shouldn't have married, and sure enough, a series of small, black bubbles erupted on his chin—a sign the man had just lied. She'd known for quite some time that Jeff couldn't be trusted with the truth, but every once in a while, his lies still surprised her. Not this time, though, so it was easy to hide her reaction.

Jeff didn't know about her gift. She would rather die than tell him.

After she'd been committed to the hospital by her father and his associates, Fin knew that she could never again trust a man with her secret. And, oh, how she'd wanted to. She longed for a world where she could collapse into strong arms, be herself, and know that she would be safe, but such relief wasn't meant for her. To confide in anyone about the things she saw… It wasn't worth the risk.

She smiled at the embodiment of her current prison. "Okay, have fun."

"Thanks, babe." Jeff leaned forward and kissed her cheek before strolling up the driveway and getting into his car.

A small pang hit Fin's heart. After a decade with him, Jeff remained quite good-looking. Like her father, he'd no doubt be one of those irritating men who'd carry his handsome looks well past middle age and into his senior years, probably be called a silver fox. Fin wasn't hideous—not even close—but she'd been called "tired" all her life, no matter how good she looked, or how well she took care of herself.

But despite his handsomeness, Jeff was no longer attractive to her—not the way he was when they'd first met, back when he was auditioning for roles (*his acting SUCKED*) and she spotted him at her favorite café. A former model, his smoldering presence and dark features had taken her breath away. He'd caught her staring at him from the register as he poured cream into his coffee from the communal pitcher.

When Jeff smiled and offered to pour some for her, she felt her cheeks color beneath the radiant sun of his gorgeousness. But this was LA, a city full of pretty ones with black hearts, so she had to be careful.

Fin blinked back tears at the memory, found herself wishing once more that she'd skipped the café all those years ago. The watered-down sludge at the office would have done her better.

AFTER SCHOOL, MARNIE would go straight from school to acting class, and then to dinner at a friend's house. Parents of the kids in the little thespian group took turns carpooling the children, a new parent each week, and if it was your night to drive, you would also host dinner at your house that evening. The other parents used these nights for extra alone-time. It was a real luxury, and it worked out pretty well, even if Fin hoped that Marnie would drop out in favor of another hobby.

Still, tonight would be one of those rare times in Fin's life that she wouldn't have to take care of anyone, so to celebrate, she wanted to do something wild and *selfish*, like go lay on the beach and read all day—or get a massage! How long had it been since she'd had a day to herself? She couldn't recall.

But such luxuries would have to wait, at least until she got her life figured out, which meant that tonight she'd be tailing Jeff.

He'd been acting weird for the past few months, those bubbles popping up more and more often, but it wasn't the lies that most troubled her; it was his anger. If he found out she had been anywhere besides at home or at work, his temper would flare. Fin knew what this was: the guilty charging the guiltless with their own emotional accusations. *Projection. Every accusation is an admission.*

Fin knew that tailing Jeff was a bad idea, and probably more than a bit self-destructive, but she *had* to know where he was going. *Just see what he's up to,* she reasoned. *Then you can finally figure out how to say goodbye. Maybe you'll get some proof that he's cheating. You can finally get a divorce and move on.*

Fin slouched down into the driver's seat of her Honda Accord and watched Jeff leave the auto body shop where he worked. He climbed into his cherry-red Dodge Charger, started the car up, and set the stereo to full-blast. Before Jeff pulled out of the body shop parking lot, Fin pulled her black hoodie over her head so as to cover her copper hair. She couldn't risk him spotting her. If he did, there would be grave consequences.

There'll be consequences soon enough, she thought. *Just not for me.* She started the ignition and began to follow Jeff's Charger from a distance, even allowing a few cars to get between them so as not to tip him off. *Subterfuge.*

Twenty minutes later, they were in Glendale. Jeff parked on the street and headed into a hotel. This couldn't be good, but it was exactly what she needed to set herself free.

THE REVOLVING GLASS doors of the hotel swallowed Fin as she entered the lobby. The interior was modern, all gleaming steel and sleek furnishings, a trumped-up IKEA palace. Polished white stone glittered beneath her feet, the floor having been augmented by a layer of sparkling rainbow fragments—of some man-made *whatever*—something plastic and fake like the rest of the city and its inhabitants.

She stayed close to the entrance and kept her head down, where she peered out from under her hoodie. A quick scan of the lobby revealed a fancy sign for Tuscan Garden, the hotel's restaurant and bar, which Fin could see from across the lobby.

At the check-in desk, a guest was arguing with one of the hotel staff, black bubbles all over the guest's heated face. But then when the hotel employee said something in return, his own bubbles cropped up.

Lies, lies everywhere. What a city.

Fin learned long ago that using her powers to argue or call out lies was a waste of time and energy. She'd have to feign discovery before presenting an opposition, which meant that she, too, would have to lie (*ugh*). Asking questions of the lying person—or worse, doubting them—only made the liar became hostile or unnerved.

In any case, it was almost never worth it to put up a fight, no matter how sad it made her.

Now, where's that lying husband of mine?

You're either upstairs already with a key to your secret rendezvous, or you're in the bar. You do like to drink.

Fin steeled herself and headed across the lobby to the restaurant. The interior design was based on Roman architecture. Tuscan-inspired columns and ferns planted in gaudy, terracotta pots where everywhere.

It's like someone ripped off The Cheesecake Factory and then added a bit more historical accuracy.

Fin scanned the tables in the room, spying several more liars before she spotted her husband at the bar. *Of course.* Jeff had saddled himself onto a cushy, leather stool next to a redhead. The woman turned toward him with a flashy smile. Fin's mouth dropped open. She was staring at a younger version of herself.

Oh God. It's real. Fin ducked behind one of the restaurant's faux pillars, heat trickling up her neck and into her cheeks. She'd been building herself up for this moment for weeks, but no matter how many times she'd told herself "*you can handle this*," the truth, apparently, felt far worse than she'd imagined.

Get proof.

Fin swiped at the tears dripping down her face and pulled out her phone. She opened her camera app and switched to video. She tapped the red record button, then tapped the screen a second time to focus the lens specifically on Jeff, the man who'd once promised to love and cherish her forever, through good times and bad, through sickness and health, until death do them part. She filmed Jeff slide his hand down his companion's lower back until it reached her rump and squeezed. Fin looked away.

I wish I couldn't feel.

When she looked back, Jeff's arm was around the woman—a tender embrace. He kissed her, slow and warm, like he used to with Fin. More tears rolled down her cheeks, falling and disappearing into the black abyss of her hoodie. The heat of humiliation painted her face. Outrage burned inside her like a bonfire. But she didn't dare make a scene. She willed herself to become stone.

Be hard and cold. Unmovable. Compartmentalize.

She focused on the recording time on her phone, the number growing larger and larger in her trembling hand.

Get mad. Let your anger fuel you. Motherfucker. I'll get you in court.

After two full minutes of this torture, she ended the recording and saved it to the cloud. She was about to pocket her phone when a notification came up on the screen: *Unknown Caller.*

What the fuck is this?

Normally, Fin wouldn't answer an unknown number, but in this moment she felt uncaring. *Reckless.* She put the phone to her ear.

"Hello?"

Click. Click. Pop. Sssssssssssssss.

The static of the call made it sound like it was coming from another planet. Fin strained to hear.

"Thingssssssss—" *Click.*

"—Are going—" *Click.*

"—To change."

Click. The call ended.

What the hell…?

The alien voice had made Fin's skin crawl. She pushed a sleeve up to find that the downy hairs on her forearm were standing at full attention.

Fin slipped her phone into her hoodie pocket and zipped the pocket shut, the video evidence she needed now secure. She took one last look at Jeff and the younger version of herself. They were still completely occupied with one another. It's like she didn't need to hide at all.

When Jeff slipped into bed close to one a.m. that night, Fin pretended to be asleep. Lying there, her cheating husband beside her, she kept cool by reminding herself, *I won't have to endure this behavior much longer.*

FRIDAY

MARNIE WAS HUMMING a kids' show theme song in the Accord's back seat when Fin pulled up to her school. Marnie usually rode the bus, but this morning, the school just happened to be on Fin's way to a very important errand, so she gave her daughter a ride instead.

"You're going to see Great-Aunt Mary?" Marnie asked, unbuckling her seat belt.

Fin watched Marnie gather her things in the rearview mirror. "Yes, Peanut," she said.

"I'm not Peanut. I'm Marnie."

Fin smiled. "All children are Peanut until a certain age, Missy, and don't you forget it."

The girl rolled her eyes, but smiled. This had been their little joke ever since Marnie was just out of diapers. "Okay," she groaned, and let loose a big sigh, pretending to excuse this enormous incivility. "I'm Peanut, but just for now, Mommy."

Fin grinned. "I thought so. Heads up, Peanut. You may be staying with Auntie for a few days while Mommy goes out of town. Is that okay?"

The girl sighed for real this time. Fin knew that sigh
had more to do with Jeff and less to do with Great-Aunt
Mary. "Why can't I stay at home with Daddy?"

The question gave Fin pause, and her smile faded.
*Because Daddy's fucking around and is irresponsible, and
I don't trust him anymore.* "Think on the bright side, baby.
You'll be able to walk to school. And I know how much
you like helping Aunt Mary at the agency."

Marnie brightened. "Yeah! I love meeting the actors and
helping pick out head shots and everything."

Fin's fading smile turned into a grin. "See? You always
have fun with Auntie!"

Marnie climbed out of the car, shoved the door shut,
and slung her backpack over one small shoulder. She
walked around the car to stand at Fin's open window. "I
know, but I'll miss you," she said, and patted her mother's
face gently.

Fin laughed. It was adorable that her daughter did
this. She knew the affectionate gesture's days were
numbered—that it would soon become embarrassing
for the girl after the sweet touches of childhood gave
way to rebellious adolescence—but this only made Fin
treasure the feeling more.

"Are you going up north again?" Marnie asked.

The Oregon coast was where Fin's mother had last been
seen alive, a number of decades ago. Fin had visited the
Oregon coast many times since her mother's mysterious
disappearance, mostly in search of clues for a cold case
that would probably never be solved, but despite her
failure to generate any substantial leads, her resolve
would never waver.

"I think I might," Fin answered. "Mommy has a lot to
figure out. But, hey, maybe next time you can come with
me. Would that be fun?"

The school's shrill warning bell rang out. Kids began running inside.

"Yeah!" Marnie kissed Fin on the cheek. "Love you!"

"Love you too, baby girl!" Fin watched Marnie disappear into the throngs of other fleeing children.

The joys of childhood innocence.

CLINK, CLINK, CLINK. Aunt Mary swirled a spoon around her mug to mix the cream into her morning coffee. "You have until I finish this, and then I have to go to work." Mary took a sip from the mug and leaned leisurely against the wall behind her.

Mary was always direct, even curt at times—like she was being now—but she was also kind in her own way, especially to Fin. In the wake of Fin's father remarrying and committing Fin to that awful institution as a teen, Mary became like a surrogate mother to her (and has since become a kind of grandmother to Marnie). Even as a kid, Fin knew that she was a burden of sorts to her mother's authoritative older sister, but it was still a relief to move in with Mary after the disaster of living with her father. As a sign of gratitude, Fin did her best to stay out of trouble. And in order to pay her way (despite it not being necessary), she would help out at Mary's casting agency, free of charge, whenever she could.

Back then, the agency was a tiny startup. Mary wasn't an actress like Fin's mother, Meredith, but she understood actors and had a keen sense for character, personalities, and stories. In the beginning, the company barely scraped by, but it was successful in its own way, providing a steady stream of actors for commercial work. At the same time, Fin's father, a well-to-do actor, was moving his new family into a Malibu mansion.

Now two decades later, Fin was back in her Aunt's home, in need of help once again.

Mary snapped her fingers. "Fin! I'm half way through this latte. Come back to Earth, please."

Many people thought of Mary as *abrasive*, one of those sharp words that had been weaponized to strip a woman of her power, but Fin had always appreciated Mary's direct approach, especially in a city where many danced around what they truly thought. People in LA often smiled right before they stabbed you in the back.

Fin folded her arms. "I need to get out of town. Things with Jeff are terrible." The image of him kissing that woman in the bar flashed through her mind, and it nearly made her cry. "I caught him with someone. Cheating. So, I need to figure out what to do next. I'm *done*." Her voice creaked on the last part.

Mary set her coffee down and pulled Fin into a hug. "Oh, honey. That son of a bitch."

Fin always got the sense that Mary never liked Jeff, only tolerated him for Fin's sake. But she didn't need to tolerate him any longer.

Mary rubbed Fin's back. "Of course Marnie can stay with me. Take as much time as you need. Do you want to stay here too?"

Fin sighed. It might actually be nice to stay. Mary had a guest bedroom with a queen mattress. Fin could haul in Marnie's twin bed, and they could share the room. It wouldn't be ideal, but it wouldn't be for long, either—just while things were in flux. "I appreciate the offer, and I may take you up on it, but only when I get back. I want to leave town, get my head back in a place where…there isn't so much chaos."

Mary's blue eyes were fixated on Fin's. "Oregon?" she asked.

"It's as good of a place to regroup as any," Fin answered, feeling small. "Better than most, in fact."

Mary watched her a moment longer, then nodded, the hard look on her face trying its best to hide the sadness in her eyes. She was used to her niece escaping to the Pacific Northwest in search of her mother's ghost, but it never made these goodbyes easier. In many ways, she would forever regret telling Fin what she knew about Meredith and Oregon. "Do what you need to," Mary said. "My door will always be open."

"Thanks. I really appreciate it."

"Well, you know how my own marriage ended," Mary muttered. "I've been there myself. Just don't forget you're family, okay? I know how you get. You don't have to shoulder all this alone. You may not have come from me, but you might as well have."

Mary squeezed Fin tight before finally letting go.

THE PUBLISHING COMPANY where Fin worked as an editor had recently begun expanding from children's picture books, chapter books, and middle-grade novels into the lucrative market of young adult fiction, which meant sitting through lots of long meetings about the direction of the new YA imprint and the complicated acquisitions process that would entail. And today was no different. But at least this time, it was a lunch meeting.

When Fin returned to her desk, stuffed with sandwich and a bit overwhelmed by all the new brand strategy, she was startled to see that her laptop had been opened and was currently displaying a real estate website that Fin had no recollection of visiting. She set down her notebook and meeting handouts, sat down at her desk, and studied the

listing on the screen. It was for a vacation home located in
Arch Cape, Oregon, one of the coastal areas of the Pacific
Northwest she loved the most. Had she mindlessly been
browsing getaways at some point and doesn't remember?
Did she leave a browser tab open after she put Marnie
to bed last night?

*Well, the place does look cool. Plus it's near the water,
somewhat affordable, and it's available now.*

Before she could read any more about the home,
the phone on her desk lit up. Jeff was calling. Another
notification told her that she had missed twelve calls.
It was rare that he called her once in the middle of the
work day, let alone twelve times. *Was Marnie okay?*

She answered. "Hey, what's—"

"I'm home with Marnie, that's what's up!" Jeff shouted.
"Where the fuck have you been?!" Fin held the phone
away from her ear. "The school's called you several times,
and I couldn't reach you, either! I had to leave work to
go get her!"

"Slow down. What's going on?"

"She's been freaking all the other kids out, telling them
a whole bunch of crazy shit—got sent to the principle.
Fin, you know I fucking hate being interrupted at work!"

When Jeff got angry like this, it became nearly
impossible to get a word in, but Fin managed. "Is
she okay?"

"I don't fuckin' know. The little weirdo is being weird,
all right? You come home and deal with this. I'm leaving
your kid here and going back to the shop." *CLICK.* He
hung up on her.

Your kid.

Bastard.

MARNIE PEERED UP at her mother, unsure of how to explain herself, so Fin, sitting beside her daughter on the couch, folded her arms and waited until Marnie fessed up. "I asked some friends if they could see Mrs. Don't," Marnie finally confessed. "I wanted to know if anyone else could see her, or if it was just me." She sighed. "It's just me."

Oh, God. This is worse than the incident last year.

Marnie had the same gift—same curse—as her mother. Fin had long suspected that Marnie had the gift, but it wasn't until last year that she knew for sure, after a panicked call from the elementary school's guidance counselor. That evening after school, Fin had to explain to the then eight-year-old Marnie that she couldn't tell others about the strange things she saw and heard.

After endless questions from Marnie, Fin finally got through to her, convinced her that, *no*, other people could *not* see faces growing black from a mold that wasn't there (Marnie saw mold instead of bubbles), and that it was in Marnie's best interest to never bring the issue up again. Things were manageable for awhile, but Fin soon found herself unable to deal with her daughter's developing peculiarities.

"Who is Mrs. Don't? Like an imaginary friend or something? What did the woman look like, Marnie? Why do you call her that?"

Marnie frowned. She moved closer to Fin and settled under her arm. While thinking about what to say next, she took a lock of her mother's hair and began twisting it into a half braid. "She wasn't much bigger than me, but she seemed like someone's mom. Her hair was wet and dark, and she was really pale. Her eyes were wrong, like she wasn't alive. There were bruises on her neck. I call her Mrs. Don't because I don't want to see her."

Fin's stomach dropped. It felt like a speeding train had just whooshed by too close, and she'd nearly fallen onto the tracks. *What the fuck do I say to this? Keep calm. She doesn't know to be afraid yet.* Fin gathered Marnie into her lap. "Do you remember what we talked about last year?"

"Uh-huh," Marnie mumbled.

Fin kissed her on the temple and rested her chin on Marnie's head. This way, she could hide her look of fear. "This is like that, but…" She tried to think of a way to put it. "*Different.* Are you scared when you see her—Mrs. Don't?"

"Not really. She's always just staring at me, and sometimes I can't see her all the way."

"What do you mean, honey?"

Marnie thought it over before replying. "It's like her face is half erased. I can sometimes see her eyes but not her nose or mouth. One time, I saw bruises on her neck, but mostly, she just looks see-through."

"So, you asked your friends if they could see her. Why? So you wouldn't feel alone?"

Marnie looked up at Fin, eyes wet, but didn't answer.

"What did the kids say?"

Marnie shrugged. "Chris laughed. Alejandro started crying. Rosa stared at me and looked afraid. Josh said I was lying, but I wasn't." Her pretty little face crumpled, and she started to cry. "I wasn't, Mom! I wasn't! I swear!"

"I know, honey. I believe you."

"That's when Mrs. Lopez got mad and sent me to the principal's office. Daddy came and was really mad and told me I was so fucking weird! I don't want to be weird, Mommy!" Marnie sobbed into Fin's shoulder and hugged her mom hard. Squeezed.

Fin fumed at Marnie's mention of Jeff. *That mother-fucker!* She wiped her eyes, then defended her husband through gritted teeth. "I'm sorry, baby. Daddy's confused. He's like the others. He—*they*—can't see things the way we do. They don't understand, my love. They can't. They never will." She stroked Marnie's hair. "This is why we have to stay quiet, keep our gift a secret."

Marnie's tears now drenched Fin's shirt.

Fin remembered the terror and chaos she felt growing up, trying to navigate her own visions and those fucking vibrations. But they had never been so powerful, nor at such a young age, as they were in Marnie. And Fin had *never* seen the dead. She swallowed a lump in her throat and hugged Marnie tighter.

I don't know how I'm gonna do this, I really don't. But I have to get out of town. But goddamn, the guilt of leaving her here is gonna haunt me.

THE SOUND OF the screen door yawning open, and the click of the lock in the front door, signaled Jeff's return home from work. In the past, that series of sounds had made Fin happy, but now there was only a feeling of dread. She didn't bother to call him to dinner.

He appeared in the kitchen doorway without speaking. His dark eyes took Fin in at the stove, then hovered over the wok of chicken teriyaki and vegetable stir-fry. He then watched Marnie doing homework at the dinner table. Furtive, the girl glanced at him without saying a word and then returned to what she was doing: coloring a map of the United States as part of a geography assignment. She pressed a blue crayon to the state of California and started scribbling.

Fin clicked the burner off. *This is going to be the last time we walk on eggshells around you,* she told herself, and slopped a melange of chicken and veggies onto a plate. She set the plate down on Jeff's table setting before serving Marnie a child-sized portion. Fin didn't take much more than that for herself. It was hard to eat when she was upset, which was becoming more often. She'd lost ten pounds that year from stress alone.

Just last week, for example, Jeff had thrown a fit when Fin had come home later than expected. It didn't matter that work had been difficult that day, or that there had been tougher-than-usual rush-hour traffic on the 405. He threw his dinner plate against the wall in protest of her tardiness, wasting food and money they didn't have. He had become used to being fed by 6:30 p.m., 7:00 at the latest. Anything after that was a problem, and it didn't matter if extenuating circumstances got in the way of his meal time. *Like the guy was incapable of snacking or feeding himself. I never signed up to be your fucking mother, too.*

When he was done being pissed about his late dinner that night, he shifted his anger to Marnie. She had made the fatal mistake of wearing her romper inside out, and Fin caught grief for it too. *How dare Fin not notice! Marnie went to school like that!* "Where is my wife's brain?" Jeff had screamed. *He finds his own rage invigorating*, Fin reminded herself. After the wreckage of that dinner, his anger spent, Jeff returned to his normal state. He talked to Fin about the news as if nothing had happened, telling her everything he thought about this or that atrocity.

What fresh Hell will tonight bring?

Fin quietly joined her family at the table. Marnie was still coloring furiously.

Jeff threw a pointed look her way. "Hey, weirdo."

The red crayon Marnie was using on her map slowed, and Marnie's face turned pink. She looked like she was about to cry.

Fin glared at Jeff. "Don't call her that."

He turned his fiery eyes on her. "Well, that's what she is." He dug into his stir-fry and brought a forkful to his mouth. "Isn't she?"

"She's a *child*," Fin stressed. "*Our child*. She deserves your love and support."

Sensing more domestic distress and knowing what comes after, Marnie's eyes widened. Watching. Listening. Impressionable.

Shit.

"Marnie, go play in your room for a bit."

The girl stood but didn't move.

"No," Jeff said. "Marnie, stay here. We're going to course correct. What you did today was fucked up." He pointed at her with his fork, then shoveled more food into his mouth. He chewed with determination.

Every accusation is an admission.

"Jeff!"

Jeff looked back to Fin. The color in his cheeks was growing redder by the second.

This isn't going to end well, Fin thought. *So be it.*

Marnie picked up her crayon again. She began moving it around the state of Idaho.

"You think this kind of behavior is okay?"

"She has a big imagination, that's all. You know she didn't actually see any of that. Why torture her?"

That's when Fin caught Marnie staring up at her mother's face. *No, not her face. Her chin. A very specific spot on her chin.*

A stab of pain hit Fin right in the heart. *She can see my lie.*

Marnie turned her attention back to her coloring, a faraway gaze in her eyes.

Is she dissociating?

Fin glared at Jeff. *I. Hate. You. For. This.*

"What the fuck are you looking at me like that for?"

Does he really expect an answer?

"This is your fault, you know," he said. "Letting her read all that weird shit, letting her watch those stupid movies and shows." Jeff inhaled more food, his teeth gnashing. "And this acting shit is going to end, do you hear me? We can't afford the classes anyway."

Fin wanted to scream but knew better. She grit her teeth so her words didn't come out of her mouth. *Those classes are free, and you know it. Mary's friend runs them.*

Marnie didn't answer. She kept coloring, the red crayon bleeding across state lines.

If Jeff hated anything, it was being ignored. "HEY!" He threw his dinner plate at Fin, but Fin ducked and it crashed against the wall behind her, shattering, food everywhere. Fin screamed.

Is Marnie all right?

She hadn't cried out in response to any of the commotion. In fact, the little girl hadn't moved, even though soy sauce had spattered some of her skin and clothes. She just stopped coloring and stared at the wall opposite her.

"How fucking weird is she?" Jeff yelled. "Just look at her! How are we going to marry her off?"

What fucking year is this?

"Excuse me?" Fin breathed.

Of course, any issue with Marnie was all Fin's fault, as if she were the only parent here. She was looking forward to the day when that became true.

A thin line of drool leaked from a corner of the girl's mouth as she stared at the wall. Then she smiled.

It was almost enough to make Jeff speechless. *How's that feel, Jeff? How's it feel to be silenced?* His mouth flapped open and closed, as if he was a fish trying to catch its dinner. Uneasy, he sputtered and grunted before he found his words.

"We have to fix this. YOU have to fix this, Fin. NOW!" His face, ears, and neck were a deep, violent purple-pink, and growing darker by the second.

Fin didn't react quick enough for Jeff's liking, so he turned and punched the wall, his fist punctuating his anger, then stalked out of the room. Seconds later, the bright tinkle of his car keys followed by a slam of the front door told Fin that he was gone. Then came the tires peeling out and the sound of his car zooming away.

Coward.

Fin looked back at Marnie. It was as if she had known bad things were about to happen and dissociated right before Jeff's explosive anger. But considering the slight cock of the girl's head and the drool running from her mouth, Fin wondered if the cause for her disassociation was something else, like the vision of…

Mrs. Don't.

"Marnie?"

Marnie giggled.

Oh fuck this. Move!

Fin scooped up her daughter and carried her to the bathroom, hoping a sensory change would snap her out of whatever was going on. She placed Marnie on the side of the tub while she readied a bath. The girl allowed her mother to take off her clothes and place her in the warm water gently, without a fuss.

Marnie threaded her hands and fingers through the water as Fin shampooed teriyaki sauce and errant bits of stir-fry out of her hair. Her daughter seemed to be on another plane of existence. Is this what spooked Jeff so much that he fled the house?

Men are dangerous when they're afraid.

Fin was also afraid. Afraid that Jeff would send Marnie away to a place with walls the color of celery, where incompetent doctors would destroy the girl's mind, just like what had happened to Fin. It had never been hard for powerful men to get rid of a *troublesome* woman. Men had long ago learned how to poison the female soul until the body just gave up and died. No direct implication in the murder. And upsetting or frightening a man, like how Marnie upset and frightened Jeff, was sometimes all it took for the man to retaliate in this exact way.

Fin shivered. *I can't allow this to go on.* She dipped a plastic cup into the bath water and poured the water over the soap suds in Marnie's hair.

The girl turned to her mother and smiled in the eeriest way Fin had ever seen.

Marnie held her stare. "Things are going to change," she said, in an odd voice too old for her body.

The cup in Fin's hand shook, and her stomach dropped, all the way down, out of her body, straight through the floor. "What?" she whispered. The cryptic voice from the previous evening's phone call had said the very same thing.

Marnie grinned and laughed. Then she took her rubber dinosaur toy off the tub's ledge and zoomed it through the water, like she used to do when she was younger. It had been a year or two since Marnie had actually played with the toy, but she insisted that it stay in the bathroom; she wasn't yet ready to part with the old friend. She looked into her mother's eyes and said in her normal voice, "Are you okay, Mommy?"

Marnie couldn't know the truth, couldn't know that her mother had somehow failed her.

"Yes, baby," Fin said. She tried her best to smile.

MARNIE GREW TIRED, and bedtime came early.

After carrying her little girl to bed, Fin pulled the dinosaur sheets up to the girl's chin, just the way she liked it. "It was a long day, yeah?"

Marnie yawned and settled deeper into her pillow. "Can I have my dragon?"

Fin retrieved the sparkly stuffed animal from the foot of the bed and placed it in her child's arms beneath the covers. She leaned forward and kissed Marnie's forehead. "Say, did you have an imaginary friend around earlier? You know, like when you were real little?"

Marnie yawned again. "You're weird, Mom." The girl then closed her eyes and went to sleep.

HOME IS WHERE you're supposed to feel safe.

Fin walked through the dining room and the mess Jeff left, and into the kitchen. She grabbed a glass from the cabinet and pulled a bottle of wine from the fridge.

Nothing like a few glasses of rosé to choke back the fear, she thought, watching the deep pink vino cascade into her glass.

She brought the wine with her into the living room and sat down on the couch, took a long gulp from the glass. She couldn't get the image of Marnie drooling out of her head, nor the cryptic way she'd spoken in the bathtub. There was no way Marnie wasn't traumatized by her father's behavior. And if Fin didn't take immediate action, Marnie would only suffer more abuse. She'd take Aunt Mary up on her offer in the morning. Nothing Jeff could do or say would stop her.

Fin downed the rest of her wine and poured another glass.

SATURDAY
(PART TWO)

FIN WOKE UP around nine that morning, to the tune of a children's television show playing down the hall. She stretched her muscles, and to her surprise, they felt sore. *No matter.* She looked to Jeff's half of the bed. It was empty.

It must be his Saturday to work. The guys at the auto body shop rotated Saturdays every month. Fin used to hate it when Jeff was gone on weekends, but not anymore. Now she was glad to have him out of the house.

Especially today.

Fin made breakfast for Marnie and packed two weeks of clothes for the girl. Her plan was to get the girl settled at Aunt Mary's, then hit the road for Oregon, where she would attempt to figure out her life.

"WHERE'S DADDY?"

Fin sighed. She hated the old refrain. Instead of answering, she just glanced in the rearview mirror at

Marnie, then pushed her sunglasses back up onto the bridge of her nose and returned her attention to the road.

"Mom?"

"He's at work, sweetheart," Fin finally replied. But what she really wanted to say was: *that asshole never came home last night.* Fin knew that Jeff would show up later, after she got home from work, and love-bomb her in an attempt to charm his way back into her life. It usually worked, but it wouldn't work this time. Fin was no longer interested in perpetuating his cycle of abuse, his domesticated version of Hell.

Marnie studied Fin's face in the rearview mirror. "Mom?" Her voice sounded hesitant.

"Yeah?"

"Last night in bed, I heard some bad noises—like a big smash and some yelling."

"What, like imaginary noises?"

"No. You and Daddy fighting."

Fin sighed. It was a mix of sadness and relief. "It was a tough day for all of us, sweet girl," she replied. "A really tough day."

"DO YOU REALLY think Jeff's at work?" Aunt Mary asked, once Marnie was out of earshot.

Fin set the girl's bags down and shrugged. "I don't really care at the moment."

In the other room, Marnie ran to Aunt Mary's open laptop and started scrolling with excitement, no doubt looking through a library of actor head shots.

"Marnie! Don't mess with that!"

Aunt Mary laughed. "Looks like I have my free intern again!"

"You're a lifesaver for watching her. I can't thank you enough," Fin said. She turned from the older woman's kind gaze. "I hope this won't be like last time."

It had been two years since the last time Fin had left Marnie with Aunt Mary, and even then, the girl was all starry-eyed about the pretty people in the computer. So, after learning how to send emails, Marnie started sending messages to actresses in the company's database, mostly to tell them they were pretty and that she hoped they would get whatever roles they were up for.

When Aunt Mary had come back from taking a phone call in the backyard, she discovered the twenty-three sent messages and spent the next hour sending follow-up emails to explain. The incident was cute and harmless but still worthy of a reprimand. *You do not touch other people's things, especially not their computers or phones.*

Most of the actresses had been fine, and most thought the message they received was adorable. One of them had a nasty stalker, however, and had worked herself into a frenzy about the security of the agency. She'd been so alarmed that she decided not to work with Aunt Mary anymore. Fin felt deeply responsible for the trouble, despite Mary's protests to the contrary. According to Mary, the woman was a flake who had never booked a job through the agency, and who no-showed at her last two auditions. Mary was glad to see her go. "*Good riddance!*" she'd said. "*The city is rife with flakes.*"

When Jeff found out about the incident, he wasn't so understanding. "*This is the first and last time I'll ever say this: You're her mother, and if you leave her again, I'll—*"

Fin shook the memory from her head.

Aunt Mary stepped forward and gripped Fin by the arms. "Get out of that darkness." She rubbed Fin's arms until she brought her out of the gloom. "Maybe when this is all settled, we'll take a breather, the three of us. How's a week or two in my Hawaiian condo sound?"

Fin blinked back tears. Marnie would love Hawaii. The first and last time Fin had been there was also due to the kindness of Aunt Mary. She'd loaned her the condo for her honeymoon with Jeff. What a different world that had been, just a decade ago. Fin sighed. A trip back to Maui *would* be incredible. And it would be healing. Sun, surf, joyous people having the time of their lives. Sailing excursions. Mai Tais. Good food. It sounded amazing. And impossible.

"Sounds like heaven," Fin said. "You're much too good to me."

Aunt Mary scoffed and hugged her niece tight. "Nonsense. It's dead at the agency at the end of the year, and I know publishing is the same way. And we both know how much Marnie loves making sandcastles. It'll be nice to have something to look forward to. Don't you think?"

"More than anything," Fin agreed.

"Then there's no debate about it. We're going." Aunt Mary nodded, then hesitated. It seemed like she wanted to say something.

Aunt Mary had the same piercing blue eyes as her sister, and when Fin looked into them, she saw her mom. To have those eyes staring back… Fin sniffed away the coming tears.

Aunt Mary frowned. "Maybe it's finally time I give you something—for your trip. It might be of some use. Wait here." Mary disappeared to her bedroom and returned a short while later with an item in her hands. It was flat and rectangular and wrapped in a tattered muslin cloth. Mary took a seat next to Fin at the kitchen table and unwrapped the soft cloth to reveal a small, leather-bound diary with faded gilding along the edges. The deep blue cover had also faded with time, as had the decorative silver stars impressed upon the leather.

Fin couldn't dare to hope, but she did so anyway. Her big, wet eyes fluttered at Mary in a silent question. "Is that…?"

Mary smiled. "It is."

Fin reached for the book, but Mary slid it away from her hand.

Jesus Christ, just give me the fucking book!!

"Finley. I've been holding this… *keeping* this for a long time. I always wondered if I should give it to you. It seems simple, right? That I should? But I've always been afraid of what this book would do to you, how it would feed your current obsession."

"But it's *my*—"

Mary raised her hand, demanding silence, and Fin promptly obliged. But still, she felt a feral need building inside her. If Mary wouldn't give Fin her mother's diary, perhaps Fin would just take it.

"That's it right there," said Mary. "That look in your eye."

Goddammit. I'm getting lectured now.

"It's that fighting spirit inside you that I'm worried about. You're so much like her, Fin. So much like your mother. And that scares me. I don't want you to fall down the same rabbit hole as her and never come back."

"You're right," Fin replied. "One hundred percent correct. Now please give me the diary."

Mary looked ready to slide the book over to Fin, but paused, her fingers pressed against the cover. "Promise me that you'll come back. That you'll come back to Marnie. Promise?"

Fin nodded and grabbed the diary out from beneath Mary's fingers.

FIN APPROACHED MARNIE in the living room. "Hey, baby. I've gotta get going, okay?"

Marnie was seated on the floor, where she had been playing on her iPad while Fin and Aunt Mary talked in the kitchen. But at the sound of her mother's voice, she dropped the tablet to her lap and looked up, with a chilling seriousness upon her face. "I'll be calling you," she whispered. The *look* in the child's eyes alluded to something Fin did not—*could not*—know. Not yet.

SATURDAY
(PART THREE)

A COOL BREEZE streamed through the car windows as Fin drove north to Oregon. Alone, the radio off, she thought about her mom, Marnie, Jeff, the diary, even work…

Dammit. Fin hated how she had to lie to her boss about why she needed to take a leave. There was never a good time to tell your boss that you were sick of being abused and needed time to sort things out before you cracked and killed yourself…or someone else. So, between sobs, Fin had blurted out that her best friend had died, and that she had to head out of state to help her friend's mother with funeral preparation.

Of course, there was no best friend. So when she caught sight of her reflection in the window behind her boss, she saw those hideous bubbles popping on her own face.

She had felt hideous in that moment.

It had been hours since she left Aunt Mary's, but still no contact from Jeff. No calls, no texts, nothing.

The plain gold wedding band Fin wore gleamed. She wanted to wrench it off her finger and wing it out the window, but she removed it and stashed it in her purse instead. It wasn't worth much, but she figured even some money would be good enough.

That's when the realization struck her. Fin was about to be a single mom to a nine-year-old girl. Guilt gnawed at her for having left Marnie behind. Aunt Mary was right. Fin *had* to come back. She couldn't abandon Marnie the same way Fin's father had abandoned her.

Even as an adult, Fin felt rage toward Theo for shirking his parental duties. He could have easily supported his daughter, but instead, she was ousted from his world for daring to exist after her mother's sudden disappearance. He supported his new family just fine with his riches, but all Fin got from him was $500 twice a year—once for her birthday and once for Christmas—and a lifetime of scorn and derision.

JUGGLING HER BAGS and suitcase, Fin flicked on the light to see a room stuck in the '70s, with brown, beige, and burnt-orange furnishings and decor. She closed the door with her heel, happy her stay would only be about eight hours. Just enough time to sleep before finishing the final segment of the road trip. Before she could put her stuff down, her phone buzzed. She hoped it wasn't Jeff.

It was Marnie.

"Hey Peanut," Fin said, locking the motel door's deadbolt.

"Hi Mommy," Marnie mumbled. Her tone was off.

"What's going on?"

"I saw Mrs. Don't again."

Shit. Shit-shit-shit-shit.

"Where are you, baby? Are you in your room at Auntie's?"

"Yeah." Then silence.

"Is she still there? Mrs. Don't, I mean." Fin peeled back the bed's comforter so as to inspect the sheets. They at least looked clean.

"I'm under the blankets. I'm afraid to look."

Well, I'm not sleeping tonight.

"How about this? I'll stay on the phone with you in case you get scared. But I need you to go and ask Aunt Mary if you can sleep in her room tonight."

"Okay."

"Are your lights on?"

"Yeah. Mommy, I don't want to see her!"

Fin's heart ached. "It's all right, Peanut. I'm here. Go ahead and pull down the covers."

"I don't want to!"

"I know, baby. But it's the only way I know how to help you right now. On three," Fin instructed. "Ready? One… Two… Three." On the other end of the line, Fin heard a rustling, a bump, and little footsteps running. Then Mary's confused voice in the background before Marnie came back on the phone.

"I did it, Mommy! I'm in Auntie's bed!"

"Great job! See? Everything's okay now. Can you get some rest?"

"I'll try. I love you, Mommy. Please come home soon."

Tears welled up in Fin's eyes for the billionth time that week. There's nothing like the guilt and pain of not being there for your child when they need you most. "I love you, too, Marnie. I'll be back as soon as I can, okay?"

"Okay."

"In the meantime, remember what I told you before I left. Don't tell anyone what only you can see, not even Auntie. All right, baby? It's important."

"I know, Mommy."

"You can always call me, but if I miss your call, please let Auntie take care of you."

After they hung up, Fin scanned the shadows in the room for a Mrs. Don't of her own. *Just in case.*

Her eyes zeroed in on her messenger bag on the floor. Within it were the manuscripts she'd promised her boss she'd work on during her leave, a binder containing photos, lobby cards, and clippings from decades past, all in relation to her mother's disappearance, and now, her mother's diary.

Fin grabbed the bag and retrieved the diary from inside. She opened the book to the first page. *Meredith Lyons* was scrawled on the name plate.

Mom.

She flipped to the first entry.

February 13, 1979

Ugh, Valentine's Day is coming up. Theo asked if I wanted to come over for dinner with Finley, some kind of friendly peace offering.

Fin's heart ached at the mention of her name.

I'd like to, but that part of my life is over. It would make me sad to be there, having a casual meal like a family again.

Let's face it, Theo still thinks I might come back to him. He parades his new girlfriends around at parties and premieres, but I know the man. I can see that look in his eyes. The longing. The hunger. Every now and then, there's a brief flash of sadness, but it's always followed by anger. Always anger. Other times, he treats me like I'm nothing more than his assistant, not his ex-wife and the mother of his child, but I guess that's what men do. They never leave you alone, energized by the hunt, or they pretend you don't exist. It's exhausting.

And it scares me.

I have plans with Harrison anyway, so too bad. Though I have to admit, Harrison is getting on my nerves too. We've only been together for six months, but I'm getting bored of his bullshit. He's needy, and he gets jealous, even when I meet Theo to pick up Finley.

How did I get myself into this mess?

So strange to read about the lives of her parents, especially the one she never knew. Fin flipped the page.

February 15, 1979

Harrison took me to a lovely dinner while Mom watched Finley.

He gave me a pair of heart-shaped gold earrings that had small, ruby stones in the centers. "To match with your favorite ring," he said.

My ring is garnet and silver. Still, it was nice, as was the Beef Wellington we ate. He must have spent a lot. I did love the romantic attention, so I made the night worth his while.

February 18, 1979

Well, that was embarrassing.

I tried to placate Theo by having lunch with him on the back lot the other day. We're both in productions with similar schedules at Peak Studios, so we met up at the commissary. It was nice. Theo didn't really pressure me too much—he was in a good mood. He said his usually irate director had complimented him on a scene that morning. Theo was actually so pleasant to be around that I... It felt like when we first met.

The problem happened when Harrison dropped in for a lunch meeting with another client. I felt his eyes on us the entire time. Can't I find just one day's peace?

At the end of our meal, we look up to find Harrison standing at the table, staring at us. Everyone knows they hate each other. I get it, I left one for the other. But Theo made his bed with all of those ingenues I found him with, and now he has to lie in it.

I must admit that Harrison is a better lover. I suspect that the same passion that drives his jealousy is the same that lights my fire.

"Damn, Mom, you were spicy," Fin said. She read on.

Theo is so cold. Sometimes I wonder if he's even human.

"What do you think you're doing?" Harrison asked. Theo stood up and protested. I couldn't get a word in, of course. I think Harrison likes provoking Theo, like he won a big prize, taking a man's wife away from him. Not that I didn't have my own say in that, but he acts like he stole me, when really, he just provided a distraction from my pain and a shoulder to cry on. And a warm body in my bed.

He gloats all the time now, and I'm tired of it. It was amusing at first. But even though I'm still mad at Theo for what he did, I can't help but pity him sometimes.

Perhaps a third option will present itself.

I've been exchanging mild flirtations with Roy, who plays my boyfriend in Running to the Sea, *which we're filming right now. He's kind. An open and generous scene partner. I'm not sure I've ever met a genuinely kind man before. I just know about the ones who use kindness as a ruse to get what they want.*

Fin felt dizzy, and the tender place beneath her sternum ached.

She was the same as her mother.

It made her sad to think that loneliness ran in the family—as did being treated poorly by romantic partners.

She laid down and wondered if her fate was already carved in stone.

No, no, and NO. This will not be how my story goes. Not any longer.

Fin yawned and tapped her phone screen to check the time. It was getting late, and she needed to get some rest before hitting the road in the morning. With reluctance, she closed the diary and put it on the pillow next to her.

"Goodnight, Mom," she whispered.

ACT 2:
ARCH CAPE

SUNDAY

TOWNS AND VILLAGES grew farther and farther apart as Fin continued her long drive north, until at last, she pulled into the rental house's driveway, crushed seashell gravel crunching beneath her tires. What a relief to put the car into park and turn off the ignition.

Sharp sea air flooded her senses as she swung the car door open and stepped out. It was evening now, and the sun had just set, but the soft glow of the porch light above the front door provided a nice, warm welcome.

Fin gathered her things and went inside.

THE LIVING ROOM looked exactly like the photos online—airy, spacious, with modern appliances and fixtures, all steel and polished stone.

If I wanted a change, I sure got one. She set down her things and explored. Next to the living room was the kitchen, and a narrow hallway led to a bathroom and a cozy little bedroom in the back. At the very end of the hall, a porch door opened onto an oceanside deck. It was too dark to see the shoreline right now, but the view would be glorious in the morning.

A bottle of wine with a gold ribbon tied around it waited on the kitchen counter. Beside it was a binder of helpful instructions and a handwritten note:

Welcome to your new favorite getaway!
If you need anything, I'm right next door.

—Charlie

How thoughtful. The Cabernet would make a lovely addition to the hot bath she planned on enjoying. What an extra-special way to relax her aching muscles and ease her tired mind. She yawned and rubbed an eye.

Fin's phone buzzed inside her pocket. Marnie was attempting a video call. Did the girl just know precisely when to ring her after a whole day on the road? Fin felt a stab of guilt over not calling her daughter first, but she had only just arrived.

Fin smiled when she saw Marnie's grinning face come up on video.

"Hi, sweetie! I just got here."

"I know, Mom."

"Okay…" Fin replied, not knowing what else to say.

"Aunt Mary and I are having fun, but I wanted to check on you after your long drive."

"I should be the one checking on you, smarty pants, but you beat me to it! Anyway, I'm tired but doing good."

Marnie giggled and looked away, distracted by a voice in the background. "Oh, we're going to make chocolate chip cookies! I'll be calling you. Bye, Mommy!"

Fin laughed. "Don't eat too many, okay? Bye, love! Be good!" They blew kisses at each other before Marnie hung up.

That girl is something, Fin thought, and placed the phone on the counter. She went to work opening the wine with the provided corkscrew.

Behind her, a clear, rippling mass floated in the air. A faint, golden light emanated from it and glinted in the glass and wine bottle.

Fin noticed the light and turned. Everything was as it had been when she entered, but she felt uneasy, as if someone was watching her. She chalked the glint up to a trick of the light and popped the cork.

Her phone buzzed again. *Marnie must have forgotten to tell her something.* But it wasn't Marnie. The caller-ID on the screen read, "Unknown." The vibrating stopped before Fin could answer.

A second later, a new voicemail waited. More than a little freaked out, Fin tapped her passcode into the phone and lifted the receiver to her ear.

Static crackled against another layer of sound—*click, click, pop, click*—like an old analog phone line clicking in and out. *Like the call a few nights ago at the hotel.* Fin turned up the volume.

"Leave… Now…" the voice warned, beneath a layer of static. Then the message ended.

Fin played it again. *Was it the same voice from before?* After a few more listens, Fin decided it was a woman's voice, but she still had no idea whose. *A new kind of phone scam, perhaps?* The message notification blinked out and disappeared, as if it had never been there in the first place.

Fuck it. I'm done caring today.

She poured herself an extra-large glass of wine.

SUDS SWIRLED AROUND Fin's skin as she eased her body into the welcoming tub. Steam ascended from the hot water and vanished into the ceiling.

Heaven is a hot bath.

Finally feeling relaxed, Fin sighed.

But something else sighed with her.

What was that?! Fin stiffened and nearly slipped beneath the water from fright. For the next few moments, she remained as still as possible while listening for the noise to repeat, but there were only the small, delicate sounds of water sloshing in the tub.

There's no one here... But I don't feel alone.

She took a deep breath to calm herself, and once again, a parallel breath echoed hers. The air hitched in Fin's throat. *Was something mimicking her? A presence of some kind? Was Fin starting to experience the paranormal, like Marnie? Was this Mrs. Don't?* Testing whatever this was, Fin exhaled, and the doubled voice did so as well—except the doubled voice sounded more like a wheeze.

Then came the unmistakable, drawn-out squeaking sound of skin rubbing against wet glass.

Fin's eyes ripped open in terror.

The mirror!

Letters had started to appear in the condensation on the bathroom mirror—written, it seemed, by an invisible finger.

What the fuuuuuuuuuucckkkkkkkkk...

The message on the glass was one word:

HELP

Fin shut her eyes again.

Nope, nope, nope, nope—I'm not seeing this.

It was all in her head. Had to be. Perhaps her childhood psychiatrists were right with their more extreme diagnoses. *Concentrate on other things. It usually makes bad images go away.*

Fin counted to sixty, then opened her eyes again. There was nothing written on the mirror, naturally.

THAT NIGHT IN bed, Fin thought more about her mother. Over the years, Fin had entertained dozens of theories regarding her mom's disappearance. *Could she have been sold into human trafficking? No, she was too well known for that.* Maybe she'd been pushed overboard during a day of yachting by someone she loved, like what happened to Natalie Wood. Or maybe she got caught up with the wrong people, fled to Mexico, and was now living under a new identity on a private beach somewhere.

But Mom had also been a Bohemian. Perhaps she'd just decided that motherhood and traditional married life wasn't for her. It was a shitty thing to abandon your kid, but not unheard of. Maybe her mom had simply given up on modern society and joined a commune. Or maybe she'd met some dashing, rich guy at a film premiere and ran away with him. That possibility didn't sound half bad.

Aunt Mary always scoffed at Fin's theories. While she agreed that her sister was free-spirited—which was common for an actress during the feminist and sexual revolutions of the '60s and '70s—she wouldn't have just up and left, especially when Fin was barely two-years-old.

That was as much as Aunt Mary would ever say though. She didn't like talking about her sister, so she rarely did. It was just too painful, and if Fin pushed her too hard, the woman would break down in tears.

JEFF GLARED AT Fin, which caused her to shrink away from him until her back hit a wall. She looked around. It was dark here, and she could see no exit. No furniture either.

Like a sound stage.

Suddenly, blood started dripping down from Jeff's hairline and over his eyes and face. He blinked, but the blink was wrong, like it happened backwards. His full attention was on her. And he looked murderous.

"I don't know where you are," he spat through the blood. "But I don't think you know where you are, either."

He made an abrupt, threatening movement toward her, but before she could run or scream, her eyes flew open.

It was dark, and she was in a strange bed, and her heart was pounding in her chest.

I'm in a rental house on Arch Cape.

She was safe, she told herself. Jeff had no idea where she was. Once her breathing returned to normal, she rolled over onto her stomach and buried her face in the pillow.

MONDAY

THE MORNING FELT blue. The color of the sky, the ocean, even the smell of the salt water. *Blue.* Along the waters, large cliffs formed from ancient volcanic rock overlooked the pleasant sand and surf. It was overcast but still lovely. Exotic, even.

Fin walked along the beach, making it a point to enjoy the peace and quiet. She had promised herself before arriving that she would take as many beach walks as the weather allowed, since isolating herself in nature—especially during the off-season when fewer people were around—reduced the risk of disturbing visions. She would see enough of those while searching for her mother in the nearby town.

Up ahead, a dog trotted over to an elderly man and dropped a tennis ball at his feet. The man clapped and stooped with a grunt to retrieve the ball, then turned and tossed it in Fin's direction.

Fin scooted out of the way right as the ball whizzed by. The dog sprinted past in pursuit.

"Oh! Sorry about that!" the man called. "I didn't see you there!"

"No worries," Fin answered. "It happens."

The older man straightened, wiped the sand from his jeans, and walked over to her. "Are you new around these parts? Or just visiting?" He seemed friendly enough.

"Visiting," Fin answered. "I'm renting a nice cottage up the way."

The dog ran back to its owner but stopped and deposited the ball at Fin's feet instead. She picked it up and tossed it.

"Thanks," the man said. "It's hard to bend down so much at my age." His eyes took her in, up and down, which made Fin glad that it was the off-season. Her body was buffered in a puffy coat, jeans, and boots. No matter the age of the man, no matter where you were, who you were, or what you wore, living as a woman always meant that you were on display for unwanted eyes.

She nodded with a smile and hated herself for it. That was the autopilot response designed to deflect, to not cause trouble. Fin couldn't exactly drop-kick a senior citizen for the small crime of being creepy.

"I'm Charlie, by the way." He grinned.

A little black bubble grew from his chin and popped.

Fin's blood ran cold. *Why would he lie about his name?* She smiled, teeth on display. Men liked it when women smiled.

A thought suddenly occurred to the man. "Wait, which cottage did you say you're renting?"

"Excuse me?"

"I'm sorry. It's just, I think it's my house you're renting—the cottage down the beach. I'm guessing you're Finley Slattery."

Fin stuck out her hand, and they shook. "Lovely home. It's a great getaway."

"That's what I've always said." The dog returned, and he patted its obedient head. "This is Moxie." He rubbed her snoot. "Keeps me company. Keeps me happy."

"I'll bet." Fin caught herself before she laughed. *Men don't like it when you laugh at them. Sometimes they hurt you for it. Sometimes for forever.* "Thanks so much for the wine! It really hit the spot after the long drive."

"Oh, no problem. Coming in from California... That's a drive. I don't miss it."

They fell into walking side by side as Charlie kept the ball toss game going with Moxie.

"Did you used to live in California?" Fin asked.

"Only about a lifetime ago," he replied. "I lived in Los Angeles until I couldn't take it anymore." He chuckled.

"Whereabouts?" she asked, keeping the conversation light.

"Hollywood. A cesspool. I can't imagine what it's like now." He glanced at her. "Did I see that's where you came from? LA?"

Her smile felt tight. "Yeah. The Valley." The dog seemed too far away. "It's an interesting place." She shoved her hands in her pockets.

"That it is," Charlie agreed, watching her a little too closely. "Are you an actress?"

"Oh," Fin laughed. "No. No way."

Charlie nodded. "Model?"

Fin shook her head and grinned through pursed lips. Aunt Mary had tried to cast her several times, but she had refused every audition. Fin had been told through-out her life that she was attractive, but she didn't feel like it. She hated thinking about her looks and couldn't imagine the searing hell of trying to make a living from something that was so fickle. The attention she received throughout her life was more negative than not, and she only wanted to be left alone. She found the Hollywood machine repellent to anyone with a soul. The fact that her mother had vanished into a Tinseltown-shaped void was the icing on the sordid cake. It killed Fin that she didn't know who was responsible. Fin also knew more than she cared to about the darker side of the industry from countless, wine-soaked nights of listening to Auntie vent.

Furthermore, Fin didn't need the nonsense in her life. There were far easier ways to make money. She was satisfied editing children's books.

"Yeah… It's a tough life. You could be in magazines, ya know," Charlie said, watching Moxie snatch the ball with her teeth.

I don't need you to validate my existence.

"You're staying up there alone, is that right?"

Do I need to sleep with a knife beneath my pillow? Guess I'll have to check for hidden cameras later!

The sound of the surf crashed somewhere beyond her. They watched each other.

Finally, he checked himself. "I'm sorry, I don't mean to pry. You have full privacy there. But if you need anything—if you just want to chat over some tea or coffee—or wine, even," he laughed, full of mirth. "Please, just call or ring the bell. I live alone and will always welcome the company."

Moxie ran up, and Charlie took the ball directly from her mouth, depositing it in his coat pocket. "But it's time I go get some rest for the moment. Afternoon naps are the best drug there is." He smiled, and she returned the gesture.

"Thanks, Charlie. It's nice to meet you."

"Until next time, then." He dipped his head in a kind of bow, straight out of another time.

She watched as he and Moxie lumbered up the beach and out of sight.

A THOROUGH CHECK of the place found no recording devices. Fin wasn't sure what to do next. The diary graced the coffee table, its cover faded with all the worn beauty of an aging Hollywood star. Fin sat on the couch across from it, staring at the book, waiting, as if it could start a conversation.

Silly. She reached over and grabbed the book, flipped to where she'd left off.

February 20, 1979

I saw the darkness bubbling up on Harrison's face.

The sentence hit Fin like a sucker punch.

No more today. She snapped the book shut and put it back on the table.

Time to go into town for groceries.

THE GAUGE ON the gas meter hovered close to empty. She could probably hold off for a few more days—she didn't plan on driving any more than she had to—but it was daylight and an independent gas station was down the road. These small towns could have funny hours. Fin pulled into the lot and came to a stop next to one of the meters. An old-school bell heralded her arrival.

Full service, read the sign on the weathered pump. *Dammit.*

The chipped door in the little garage's office opened. A man in an oil-stained jumpsuit dragged himself out and peered at her. His face looked as battered as his gas station, lined with deep creases. His eyes were nestled within the leathery pouches of his skin, nearly black beneath spidery brows. He was maybe in his seventies. It was hard to tell. He didn't seem to have ever worn a drop of sunblock in his life.

Fin pushed a lever on her door, and the window whirred down. She stopped it halfway.

"Hello there, miss," the gas station owner rasped, straight out of Central Casting. "Fill 'er up?"

Will he warn me not to go near the woods or a cursed lake? "Yes. Please. Unleaded." The embroidered name patch sewn on his uniform read *John.* He watched her in the car's side mirror for the entire excruciating time it took to fill the tank. *This place isn't as charming as usual. Maybe this will be my last trip.*

Perhaps this was a good time to check in on Marnie. Fin took her phone from the cup holder, tapped in the passcode, and clicked on her text message thread with Marnie.

Hi baby! How are you doing today? I miss you!

Hi Mom! I'm in art class, can't talk.

Oh, right. Monday. Love you, Peanut! Going into town. Will find a treat or two to bring home. I'm here if you need me. xoxo.

Fin looked up to see John still staring. *Dammit.*

"I don't know how you people stand it, all that electronic nonsense," he said.

Of course you're one of those guys, John.

"The government tracks everything you do, you know. No privacy." He didn't seem to understand that he was violating hers right now. He glanced at the pump and wiggled the handle a few times, herding the last few drops into her tank. Satisfied, he screwed the gas cap back on, pushed the panel back in, and waddled back to her. "Cash? Cash is always better, you know. They can't track that, and we don't have to pay taxes on cash. By the way, you should stop using that 5G if you have it." He pointed at the phone in her hand. "It'll make ya sick. Kill ya!"

Fin wondered how it felt to be so sure of oneself, and so positively wrong at the same time.

"I haven't seen you here before. You're not from around here, yeah? Just move in?" His breath was like an acidic cloud that wafted up into her nostrils. She turned away from the smell and searched for the wallet in her purse. If she got sick or dropped dead, it'd be due to this idiot's stench. "Did you say cash?"

"Yes, honey. Cash is the greatest thing in this great land." His eyes skimmed over her body.

Ugh. She was going to need another bath. Thankfully, she actually had the amount owed. She couldn't snatch the bills out fast enough. She forked them over through the open window. "Keep the change."

John grinned to show a mouth of yellowed teeth. "God bless America!"

Fin turned on the ignition and drove away.

AFTER DINNER BACK at the house, Fin pulled out her laptop and got to work on one of the manuscripts she'd promised to give notes on, but she didn't get far. The diary called to her. It was small but powerful, and it needed her in some way, needed to be read.

She poured a glass of wine, grabbed the diary, and headed out to the deck. A welcoming pink-orange sunset colored the sky. *Beautiful.* Fin made herself comfortable on a cushy patio chair and opened the book.

February 23, 1979

He's still lying to me about something. I hate this gift, or curse, or whatever it is. It's taxing. I have to say though, it's kind of helpful in Hollywood to know when people lie to you!

I just wish I could turn it off sometime, so that I don't have to see it everywhere.

I'm not sure what the lie is, but Harrison's probably seeing someone else, as I've been cooling off with him. It could be that he's lying to me about a role in some upcoming project, I don't know.

At least it's been a while.

I often saw the darkness gathering on Theo's face every time he said he was with a friend or at a meeting. Of course, he was with another woman instead.

I've never told anyone about this, for obvious reasons. Ha ha, if anyone ever finds this diary, they'll think I'm insane.

I'll burn this book when I finish it. It'll feel cathartic, like when I torched the other diaries.

Aunt Mary mentioned once that Meredith had been "touched"—saw and heard strange things—and now, having it confirmed by her mother's own writing, Fin wondered if hearing and seeing things that others could not had something to do with her mom's disappearance.

Fin and Marnie weren't alone. Turns out, these little waking nightmares ran in the family.

TUESDAY

IT HAD BEEN far too long since Fin had come to this hidden time-warp of a town, searching for herself while peering into the past for her mom. With its little winding roads and small population, this place was so calm and quaint—so unlike the helter skelter of LA.

Her first stop was the local bookstore, Book Haven. The front of the store was as to be expected. Fiction on one end, non-fiction on the other, and a small check-out area filled with candy, toys, and gifts. The back of the store, however, was reserved for antiques. Iris, the elderly shop owner, was known to scour the internet for imported oddities, like surrealist paintings and Victorian hair art.

Iris stood behind the counter, pricing a stack of candles and books when Fin entered. She was a cheerful woman in her seventies, with long white hair and a wry outlook. Fin knew from speaking to her on a previous trip that the woman had bought the place after finding it on vacation decades ago.

I could be so lucky.

After the previous owner had passed away, the future of the store was in peril. The deceased owner's two children had lives of their own in other parts of the country and were unmotivated to carry on the store's legacy. They just wanted to sell the building as soon as possible. Having been dissatisfied with her secretarial job at the time, Iris decided to make an offer, and to her surprise, it was quickly accepted. She upended her entire life for a new start, and built the bookstore into a storied destination for travelers and lovers of uncommon goods. Fin couldn't help but envy the old woman.

Imagine leaving everything you knew, starting over, burning your whole life down to build a better one.

Fin waved to Iris and headed straight to the vintage section. Crates of books and magazines of various decades sat next to a lamp crafted from brass in the shape of an anchor. Several empty picture frames were stacked against two shelves filled with bric-a-brac, like harlequin figurines made of porcelain and colored glass ashtrays.

A display case of antique costume jewelry and purses of different fabrics and leathers caught her eye. Although she wasn't in the market for any of that, Fin knew that Marnie would enjoy playing dress-up with the sparkling jewelry. She combed through a pile of dangling earrings and bracelets to see if she could find a matching set, but after coming up empty, settled on a few antique necklaces made of rhinestones. She wondered about the previous owners.

What were those people like? Who might they have been during their time on Earth? And where had they gone? Had they been snuffed out forever? Or had their souls gone on to new adventures?

A humming sound, steady and low, invaded her thoughts. It sounded almost like a refrigerator. Fin looked around, but she couldn't find the source of the noise.

Oh, no. Not this again...

It was rare that she heard objects vibrate, but when they did, things tended to get mysterious. As a child, she'd once found an old Rolodex in her father's office that had hummed. She'd gone to open it, curious to what she might find within its rotating cards of names, addresses, numbers. Some cards contained lewd, handwritten notes—such as *best head in Hollywood, massive tits,* and *will fuck anyone for a role*—but the mysterious markings were the big black Xs in the top right-hand corner of some cards. Fin got a terrible feeling about those black Xs. They had been made with such violent strokes. She'd never be able to explain why, but those Xs had felt infused with death. As Fin stared at them, horrified, transfixed, her dad—*Theo*—rounded the corner, screaming that she shouldn't be in his study, touching things. He'd ripped the Rolodex from her hands and locked it in a desk drawer before escorting her from the room and locking the door behind him.

Back in the bookstore, Fin listened to the quiet hum some more. Her shoulders dropped. *Fine, let's figure out where this thing is.*

Near one of the crates, the sound grew louder. She crouched down, and the humming amplified. It was coming from inside the crate. She stuck her hand in and fished around until a whisper of electricity buzzed against her skin. She jerked back. A new sensation. The vibrations, though rare, had never *stung* her before. It was alarming, but she had to know what this was. She reached back into the musty stack, grabbed the startling object, and yanked it from its hiding place.

In her hand, she held a tattered magazine, its edges yellowed from age. It was an old copy of a defunct Hollywood gossip rag called *Whispers*, dated July 1979.

Her mother's most famous head shot graced the cover, beneath the ominous headline: *MISSING!*

Oh God. Fin felt lightheaded. The magazine buzzed in her hand. She staggered to a well-used armchair in the corner and nearly collapsed onto the seat. She slumped into the chair and rubbed her scorching face.

"Are you okay, dear?" Fin looked up to see Iris. The woman looked concerned. "Do you need some water?"

"Yes, that would be wonderful."

Iris left and then returned with a mug of cold water, which Fin chugged down. She then held the empty mug against her face, using the chilled porcelain to cool her cheeks. Slowly, she felt herself coming back to life.

"Better?" Iris asked.

"Yes, thank you." "Hey, I know this is going to sound weird, but"—she held up the copy of *Whispers*—"have you ever seen this woman around town? It would have been decades ago." Fin felt silly even asking, but she had to try.

"The missing actress? No, that happened just before my time here. You know what? You kind of look like her."

A bittersweet smile formed on Fin's lips. She flipped through the magazine to the cover story. A sidebar on the magazine spread was titled *Ex Loves.* The column featured one of her parents' wedding photos, and a "*last seen with*" shot of her mother with some guy named Harrison Bentley, in the parking lot of Musso & Frank. The name sounded familiar. Had Fin seen his name at some point, somewhere in her clippings?

"Have you ever seen either of these guys?" she asked Iris.

Iris took the magazine. "Huh. No, I can't say that I have." She handed it back to Fin. "That guy in the parking lot looks a little familiar, though. I can't place him. Is he an actor too?"

Fin studied the photo. The guy looked to be in his thirties or forties, but it was hard to say. He was clearly angry at the time of the photograph, and looked about ready to attack the photographer.

"I think he was," Fin replied.

"Why the interest? You one of those true crime fans?"

"I guess you could say that," said Fin."I'd like to purchase this one, if you don't mind."

"It's there to be sold. Say, if you're looking for more information about that case, there are some folks around town that would remember a woman like that."

"Would they talk to me?"

"Darling, old folks around here love nothing more than to talk, especially to inquiring strangers. Most days, they don't have an audience."

GRIPPING THE PAPER bag that held her Book Haven purchase, Fin headed over to Arch General.

The people inside were unhurried and kind—character traits that were unthinkable in the city. She flashed back to the chaos of every Trader Joe's parking lot she'd been to in LA and shuddered. Was friendliness the result of living in Arch Cape?

Arch General was owned by the Malerman family: Joe, Sadie, and Chris. Fin recalled Joe and Sadie from her last trip. One of them ran the bakery while the other manned the front counter, and they traded roles on a whim. If you were lucky, you could get one, maybe two baked items before they sold out. The store also had a coffee bar, but the only additives it offered were 2% milk and cream. No almond, soy, coconut, or oat milk in these parts.

Joe's younger brother Chris ran the deli with a friendly smile. Fin wasn't sure how slicing meat and cheese and making sandwiches for people all day could make one so happy, but the conviviality was nice.

After a friendly chat, Fin showed Chris the pictures from the old magazine, but he didn't recognize her parents or the guy with her mom. He did, however, wish her luck on her search.

Fin did some quick shopping for foodstuffs, then headed over to the checkout counter to purchase her items and speak with Joe.

"Good evening, young lady," Joe smiled. "Find everything you're looking for?"

Fin's breath stopped. She never noticed before, but Joe looked a lot like the Harrison guy from the magazine. She felt her face getting hot, similar to how she felt in Book Haven. Her toes tingled, and she gripped the counter for support. "Yeah," she breathed. She stared at a bag of tortilla chips poking out her basket to minimize the sudden feeling of vertigo, and in hopes that she would soon regain her focus.

"You okay there, hon?" Joe asked.

Fuck. Could this really be the same guy?

"I think so, thanks. I probably just need to eat something."

Joe chuckled. "Low blood sugar is no joke! Why don't you grab one of these?" He gestured to a display of artisanal truffles near the register. "They're made by a chocolatier up north." He leaned in with a conspiratorial grin. "Worth ever calorie." He patted his round belly and laughed. "I'll give you a discount on them. What do you say?"

The truffles *did* look tempting—dark chocolate bonbons on display in a little box. One box was tied with a violet satin ribbon, the truffles within painted with edible ink designs. Some had honeycomb graphics, others were decorated with raspberry crumbles and little golden swirls.

"No thanks, Joe."

Joe opened the box, retrieved a chocolate with a flower design, and handed it to Fin. "Here. Try a free sample first."

Fin took the chocolate and popped it in her mouth. It did taste delicious.

"Good, ain't they?"

Fin nodded and chewed some more.

"Feel better?"

"I do, actually," she lied.

Joe laughed. "Glad to hear it. Nothing like a little chocolate therapy." He continued to ring up her groceries. "Anything else I can help you with?"

Fin pulled *Whispers* from the paper Book Haven bag, the magazine already opened to the cover-story spread. She discreetly compared the picture of Harrison to Joe.

Joe does resemble him. But maybe I'm too eager to find a connection.

Fin cleared her throat. "This is going to sound silly, but have you ever seen any of these people here? I know it's been a long time." Fin put the magazine down on the counter for Joe to see.

Joe squinted. "Hold on. Let me just get my glasses." He fetched the bifocals dangling from the chain around his neck, perched them on his nose, and studied the photos in the magazine. His reaction was small, barely noticeable, but Fin saw his pupils widen just a bit and the muscles around his eyes twitch. "Hmmm," he said. "Hard to say."

A number of small black bubbles boiled up on his forehead.

Joe turned and called out to his wife. "Sadie! Come over here a quick second, will ya?"

When Sadie arrived, Joe handed her the magazine.

"Have you ever seen any of these people?" He scratched his chin. "What year was this, anyway?"

Fin answered. "Spring, 1979."

Sadie considered the old photos and chuckled. "That's a long time ago! With all the vacationers we get, it's hard to remember folks from last summer, let alone 1979. But I'm certain I would have remembered a famous actress had I met her. We don't get many Hollywood celebrities up here in Arch Cape."

A little black sphere bubbled up on her cheek and popped. Fin swallowed and put the copy of *Whispers* back in the paper bag. Under the eyes of the proprietors, she felt flushed again. Dishonest behavior had a way of doing that to her.

"You related to any of them?" Sadie asked, echoing Iris. "You kind of look like the lady there." Joe bagged the remainder of the items.

Don't give yourself away. A lie for a lie.

Fin shook her head. "Book research. True crime. Missing persons cases, specifically. Thanks anyway."

In the cigarette-branded mirror behind the counter, Fin saw the oily black bubbles popping on her face. Before shame got the better of her, she dug out a credit card and tapped it on the reader.

"Are you gonna be in town for a bit?" Joe asked. "We can contact you in case we remember anything."

"No need. I'm sure I'll be back in at some point." She smiled. "Have a great day."

"Come back anytime," Sadie said, her face dripping with the invisible oil.

BACK AT THE rental, Fin settled in with a fresh bottle of rosé and an old phone book from 1995 that she found in one of the kitchen drawers. Using the Yellow Pages, she made a list of other people in town that she could interview about her mother.

The list ended up being pretty short—most of the listed businesses no longer existed—but it provided a few decent leads: Roberto Hull, a librarian; Justine Golden, a veterinarian; and John Lawson, the paranoid owner of the gas station Fin had visited the day before. Fin recalled the man's foul smell and shuddered. And of course, there was still Charlie Moorehead, the rental owner from the beach.

Fin drew her legs up onto the couch and into a crisscross position. She wondered if she should just hire a private investigator, or if it would even be worth it.

She picked up her phone and texted Marnie instead. *How's my baby doing? I love you!*

A minute later, Marnie wrote back: *I'm at a casting session, Mom! It's super fun! I just have to be quiet.*

That's wonderful, honey! Excellent. Be sure to pay attention to the feedback Aunt Mary gives the actors.

I will, Mom! Gotta go. I'm listening.

Fin smiled. *Nice job. <3*

She placed her phone down, happy that Marnie was doing well.

Fuck it. She'd get nowhere if she let fear win. She snatched the diary from the coffee table and started to read.

March 1, 1979

Harrison punched Roy in the face.

Fin nearly snorted wine out of her nostrils. "Well, holy shit," she murmured, and continued reading. She tipped the rest of her glass back and set it on the table.

Sarah, our makeup artist, had to work her magic to cover up the black eye, I tell you.

Harrison had dropped by set, and we happened to have been shooting a love scene. It was a hot one, too, with Roy and I just about buck naked beneath the sheet.

Wow, that man… I felt him against my leg as we got heavy into it for the camera. I'm kind of intrigued to learn more, shall we say.

"Mom!" Fin gasped, chuckling.

The best part was that Roy was very gentle and kept checking in to make sure I was all right. None of my co-stars have ever done that before. He is an intoxicating blend of intensity, sexuality, and kindness. Wow. I wouldn't be surprised if he became a movie star very soon.

Well, Harrison happened to be standing behind some of the crew, watching from the shadows. When the scene ended, he waited until Roy was walking to his dressing room in nothing but a robe. Harrison sucker-punched Roy and knocked him to the ground. One of the grips grabbed Harrison and pulled him away. Roy was shocked. You don't expect to get bum-rushed after a love scene.

"How dare you!" Harrison screamed at him.

"How dare I what?" Roy retorted, in the most extraordinary English outrage I've ever heard. "Do my job correctly? At least I can act, you legendary failure! Though with Merry here, I don't have to."

My God. I almost screamed.

Roy laughed as Harrison turned red. He tried to rush at Roy again, but Roy sidestepped this time and—*I'll never forget this*—SLAPPED Harrison across the face! It made the most satisfying CRACK sound. Roy couldn't have been more English about it unless he'd backhanded him with a leather glove and challenged him to a duel, a-ha-ha. Then a gaffer and a PA stepped in to help our grip. They held Harrison there before security arrived to escort him off the set... and off the back lot. For once, both our director and producer were SPEECHLESS.

It should have been a closed set.

Roy and Harrison hadn't met before this altercation, but everyone apparently knows the story behind that "legendary failure"—including me now. Harrison used to be an actor, but he wasn't great. He was one of those guys who failed up until he couldn't. His readings were wooden, and he had trouble listening. He never inhabited the role, never came off as natural. You could always tell that he was waiting to speak his lines. It made him not just a bad actor, but a terrible scene partner. Sometimes he was okay, sometimes laughably bad, but always kind of excruciating.

What Roy referred to—the event that forced Harrison to leave acting and go into management—was the time Harrison was on set with a poor actress who had to put up with too much of his nonsense. The director—who cast Harrison only because of a favor to the producer—had even started giving him line readings, for Christ's sake. Anyway, they were shooting a love scene similar to the scene with Roy and myself, their characters lying in bed post-coitus, supposedly in love.

Harrison took it too far. His hands went everywhere, including down the panties of his co-star, who broke character and screamed.

He didn't know that she was dating the producer of the picture, who was just ten feet away. Harrison said it was for realism, to get both of them in the mood. He complained that he wasn't getting what he needed from her in the scene and decided to go "Method."

I know of plenty of handsy actors, but none of them were ever stupid enough to try such a move on set while rolling. He's not a director like Bertolucci or Polanski. Harrison's been pretty much blacklisted from acting ever since. I just hate that I'm only discovering this shit now. I feel like an idiot, like I should have known.

But isn't that what most women say? Like it's our fault, like we could have prevented this? No, the fault lies with them.

I'm going to have to find new representation. This is getting embarrassing, and I'm really starting not to like Harrison much. I didn't know anything about this story until today, so I needed to find out more. I asked our costumer if she knew what Roy was talking about during a fitting. I wish I hadn't, but it's better to know something like this. How can you trust a guy like that? I've made some piss-poor decisions, apparently.

Roy is really something rare. After Harrison was escorted away, he gave me a funny, conspiratorial look, then asked if I was okay. What a gentleman! I said yes, I was fine, and thanked him. The nickname "Merry" probably made me blush. It must have. Or I just reacted well to his chivalry. I can't recall a man ever looking out for me before.

I might be in trouble.

March 3, 1979

Roy calls me "Merry" any time he speaks to me now, and I feel a shy smile on my face every single time.

Better yet, he asked me to dinner. I'm elated!

Fin shook her head in disbelief. Mom had as much drama off-screen than on, it seemed. She continued on to the next entry.

March 7, 1979

Roy Treadwell is a gentleman and has an enormous cock. And talent, too!! He does something wild to me. I feel like I've won the goddamn lottery.

Fin burst out laughing. She wished she had known Meredith. They could have had some hilarious conversations. She flipped the page.

March 10, 1979

I've been a naughty girl, seeing both Roy and Harrison. Why do men get to have all the fun?

Well, if I'm being honest with myself, I'm a little scared to break it off with Harrison. I've been slowly pulling away, making myself scarce more often than not. This way, he gets used to the idea of ending things gradually.

We went to Musso & Frank last night. I wish I hadn't, but I wanted to break up with him in person. It's usually better that way. And…sometimes it's not. A few drinks in, he got dark, both in mood and with some of that awful, bubbling face decay stuff that I hate seeing. Lies. Lies, lies, lies, goddammit. I wish I could talk to someone about what I see, but it makes Mary so uncomfortable, and I don't know if I can trust anyone else. I don't think those drinks were his first of the night, either.

I'm a watered-down version of my mother, Fin thought.

He noticed I was quiet. But what was I supposed to say to all of the grumbling? I'm not sure I care to soothe away his feelings. He's just so angry and doesn't take responsibility for anything, least of all his emotions. And it always feels better to look away from the darkness slowly eating his skin—the darkness that no one else can see. It's frightening.

But then Harrison got maudlin. He knows he's losing me. He knows I've been seen around town with Roy (quite joyously, too), thanks to those damn gossip rags and a few loose-lipped "friends." I told him that I was unhappy, that he's been driving me away, and that things aren't working out between us.

He begged me to stay. Told me I was beautiful, wonderful, and talented. He said that I would go far, and he could see it coming. He's heard more about the work we're doing on Running to the Sea *(since getting banned from set), and how he can't wait for the film to come out. He said my career is going to skyrocket.*

And then he said he loved me, that he wants to be with me always. It would have broken my heart if it hadn't been so occupied with lovely, magical Roy. Still, I felt bad. But he'd had his chance.

It's not my fault you're a dick, man.

We were photographed in the parking lot by some annoying bottom-feeders. They somehow found out about the altercation between him and Roy on set and have been following us ever since. The mood turned again, with Harrison yelling at them and threatening to hurt them. They ate that up, of course, and tried provoking him more. He ended up shoving one of them and grabbed another guy's camera.

Harrison smashed it on the pavement and we drove away. But the film inside it is probably fine, and the photographer will get paid for this nasty business. I will never understand why some people just can't let others be, entertainment industry or not.

I don't know what to do. Mom has disliked him for a while now, and talking to her about it only gets me "I told you so" and "Well, what did you think would happen with a man who'd break up a family?"

Last time, she told me that I deserved what I got.

Maybe I do. Maybe I fucking don't.

Fin shook her head. *That was harsh.* But she also knew that motherhood was hard. She hoped she was as kind to Marnie as she was able.

April 1, 1979

Things have been heating up with Roy—who's a joy! He's funny and wonderful in every way. Trust me, I've been looking for flaws, but I can't find them. At least not yet. And I love working with him.

We've been kissing more than necessary for our scenes, but it really adds to the film! Chemistry, ya know? These are real kisses, real emotions. I love the way that he looks at me. I feel ticklish in certain places, too.

This could really be something. Dare I dream after so many nightmares?

April 13, 1979

Today was Finley's second birthday.

"Cheers," Fin said and poured herself more rosé. "Happy birthday to me." She relished the wine, but didn't feel so joyful.

The focus should have been on her. Instead, I had to deal with all three men in my life—past, present, and hopefully future.

We had planned to throw a chill soirée at Sandy's house, my new friend and co-star, who very kindly offered to host a birthday celebration, but it turned mostly into cast pool party. I'm glad that Finley is still so young she can't tell what's going on in the world, but I feel guilty about what happened.

Like everyone else there, I had had too much to drink by the time Mom brought Finley. I hate how guilty she makes me feel over watching her while I work and figure out what the hell I'm going to do with my life. It'd be so grand if I could afford a nice estate someday with a guesthouse. One of those mother-in-law cottages where I could have Mom or even Mary there full-time. I'd love to be rich enough one day to put one or both of them on the payroll. They wouldn't have to work shitty jobs. They could hang out, live their lives, and could watch Finley during filming and whenever Theo's busy, which is always.

Speaking of, Theo ended up bringing some tarted-up model/actress/whatever to the party. I know that his looks and money aren't nearly enough to make up for his bullshit, and whoever this new girl is, she'll realize that soon, too.

I caught him staring at me so many times. Ugh. Typical. He's starting to freak me out, though.

His eyes were filled with hatred at one point—when Roy was sitting with Finley and I. She was on my lap, and I was feeding her apple sauce while feeding myself a mimosa (heavy on the champagne). Don't judge me, Diary, I've had a lot to deal with lately. Roy had just given a lovely stuffed kitty to Finley, and she was fussing over it. So nice of him. He was very sweet, fawning over us. I still can't get over how wonderful he is.

Fin swallowed the dregs of her second glass. She still had the worn, orange-and-white stuffed kitten, tucked away in her nightstand. She'd thought it was one of the only things her mother had ever given her. Had been *able* to give her. At least the toy had come from someone good, someone who could have made all the difference in their future. *If Mom had been allowed to have one.* Fin blinked away tears, refusing to ruminate too much. She continued reading:

And then out of the corner of my eye, Theo raised his finger like it was a gun. He aimed it my way and made a shooting motion, just like Charles Bronson at the end of Death Wish.

"Jesus," Fin breathed. She'd seen that film, and while Bronson was considered the hero in it, making that gesture to anyone in real life under the kind of circumstances her mother had been in… *That was nothing short of a threat.*

Fin wondered. *I could turn the diary over to LAPD's cold case division, if there is one.* She didn't know how homicide departments worked, if there was even anyone assigned to the impossible tasks of finding murderers several decades in the past. The cops would probably laugh at her. But a documentary filmmaker wouldn't. She made a mental note to ask her coworkers if any of them knew such filmmakers. Fin could even put up some money to fund the project—she scoffed at herself. *What money??* She sighed, putting the idea on the back burner of her mind, and went back to reading.

I don't think Theo knew that I was watching him beneath my sunglasses. That hooker was on his arm, getting wasted

*with him, and I felt his glare when Roy touched my knee
and kissed me on the cheek. He'd told me how beautiful
I looked.*

*As lovely as that was, Theo made the day ugly. He was
watching the three of us. He looked like he wanted to kill me.*

Fin shivered. She'd been on the receiving end of similar torturous looks from Jeff. She wondered how many
countless other women had endured them throughout
history. What was the ratio for those who had lived to
those who had been killed? What were the factors that
had pushed men over the edge into murder? It was a
terrifying phenomenon.

A puddle rippled in the air above her head. She jerked,
a full-body spasm, the diary falling to the floor. A small
beam of golden light emanated from the puddle and
reached down to touch the glass screen of her phone.

What-the-fuck? What-the-fuck? What-the-fuck?

Her phone buzzed.

Unknown, read the caller ID, just like before.

Her insides twisted, but despite her growing apprehen-
sion, she swiped to answer.

Click, click, pop, click, fizzed in her ear.

It sounded impossible, too far away to reach, like a call
from the dead—from one dimension to another.

"You're not safe," a voice told her. And then the line
went dead.

She rubbed her eyes in exasperation. *Maybe Gas Station
John was right about 5G phones.*

Fin poured another glass of rosé and chugged until it
emptied. Alcohol helped dull the visions. She hissed out
a breath from the burn in her throat.

Wherever they had come from, the phantom phone
calls had kicked the door open on this reality. Or maybe

Fin had finally gone off the deep end. All these sights, sounds, sensations—they were all just in her mind.

Jeff's voice echoed in her head: *"You're crazy."*

Fin shoved away the unwelcome memories of Jeff yelling at her, of his huge mouth barking without sound. She imagined wadding up his face like a piece of paper and then lighting the ball on fire.

WEDNESDAY

FIN SAT IN at the kitchen table and jotted notes in a manuscript for work. A freshly poured cup of Earl Grey tea steamed next to her hand, waiting to be enjoyed. Beyond the cup of tea was the kitchen window, and beyond that was the familiar sight of Charlie walking Moxie down the street.

Moxie stopped to sniff something, and Charlie turned to look at the rental house. It almost appeared as though he knew he was being watched. He squinted. *Could he see her?*

But that's when Moxie spotted something else of interest—a bird, maybe—and pulled hard at her leash. Charlie let himself be led away, and they disappeared from view.

Fin felt an urge to follow them. She took a quick sip of tea and headed for the door, grabbing her jacket on the way out.

She followed Charlie from a distance. Every now and then, Moxie would sniff something else or relieve herself, and these pauses gave Fin opportunities to study Charlie's profile. At times, she'd lift her sunglasses to peer at him. He did look somewhat like her mom's old manager, but

Arch General's Joe Malerman looked like Harrison even more. But unless the men allowed DNA testing, Fin could only ever speculate.

What the hell am I doing? This is useless.

Fin sat down on a bench that overlooked the beach. The waves rolled and crashed in the distance, cool sea air licking at her face. She zipped up her jacket and stuffed her hands into her pockets.

The soft crunch of footsteps on dirt.

Fin spun around to see Charlie standing behind her. Moxie's tail wagged. "Hello again. Mind if I join you?"

"Uh…sure. I don't own the bench."

Charlie took a seat beside her. "Sit, girl," he said to Moxie, and fished a dog treat out of his pocket when she obeyed. The dog lapped the fake bone from his hand and crunched it in her mouth. Her tail swept the ground as she watched her master, eager for more.

"How are you enjoying your stay, young lady?" Charlie asked.

"It's wonderful, thank you. It's been great to clear my head." Fin looked out at the sea. Faint rays of sunshine poked through heaping clouds and reflected on the water, which sparkled.

"That it is," Charlie agreed. "This area's a wonderful place to start over."

Fin looked back at him. "I've been thinking of doing exactly that—moving here."

Charlie shifted in his seat and glanced at her. He turned his attention back to Moxie and patted her head. "Oh?"

"Yeah," Fin said. "I don't know if I want to raise my daughter in LA."

He looked back at her, studied her face. "I hear ya. Once upon a time, I imagined differently, but it wasn't meant to be. No matter. I'm much happier here. It's a simpler life."

"Seems so."

Fin tried to remember the shape of Harrison's face in the magazine, whether his jawline was sharp like her father's, or more rounded. She wished the photo hadn't been printed in black and white. She would have liked to compare hair and eye color.

"This place has everything I think we need," Fin continued. "A book store, general store, post office… A gorgeous beach. Yeah, we could be happy here."

Charlie leaned forward to stretch, but he kept his eyes trained on Moxie. "That's wonderful. Well, I'm gonna get this one back home and fed." He nodded toward the dog. "Got some errands to run." He got up and half-bowed without looking at Fin. "Enjoy yourself."

She waved, just in case the movement attracted his attention—*let me see those eyes*—and watched him go.

THE ARCH CAPE Public Library was small and cozy, located just a few minutes drive from Book Haven and Arch General.

An elderly man—probably in his eighties—stood behind the information counter. He had a head full of white hair and wore a smile beneath his bifocals. He seemed nice enough. "May I help you?" he asked.

Roberto Hull, read his name tag. Fin smiled.

"I hope so." She pulled *Whispers* from her bag and opened to the now-familiar pages. "I'm doing research for a book about missing persons, and this case is the one I'm currently working on. Unfortunately, there isn't much to go on. I don't suppose you've ever seen any of these people here, once upon a time?"

Roberto took the magazine. "Hollywood people, hmm?" He considered the photos. "Anything's possible," he murmured. "But I can't say that I've come across them, neither then nor now."

No lies detected. Fin took the magazine back and re-sheathed it. "I appreciate it."

"You're welcome to search the library's public records. Everything is digital now. No more having to comb through old newspapers or microfiche. Just let me know the months and years you'd like to search, and I can get you set up."

I fucking love libraries.

FOUR HOURS LATER and Fin was more frustrated than before. She'd combed through pages of news from 1979 through 1985, but found nothing that provided more insight into her mother's disappearance. At one point, Fin came across an article for the opening of Justine Golden's Happy Arch Pets Clinic—all the way back in 1981, when the woman first moved to the area—but that story also led nowhere.

More interesting were the many arrest reports for John Lawson, the gas station owner. He'd been placed on the National Sex Offender Registry in 1989 for a heady blend of public exposure, urination, and intoxication at a local children's playground. Lawson was arrested several times after that, but never for something so disturbing. He was reported as being drunk during every arrest, and after a series of DUIs, his license was finally revoked.

Fin thought back to the gas station. The garage was connected to another small building, a house that he worked out of and no doubt lived in. She wondered what she'd find in there if she were to…take a look around while he slept.

She thought again about Justine Golden. Maybe it was time to pay the woman a visit. She opened a web browser on the library computer and searched the clinic's name. She clicked on the first returned URL for the clinic's website and frowned when she saw the sad message plastered at the top of the website's homepage:

Dear Patients,

Dr. Golden unexpectedly passed away yesterday, and all appointments for this week have been canceled. For urgent calls, please contact the Arch Cape Animal Hospital. The clinic will continue operating under her daughter's care next week. Thank you so much for your patronage.

The family asks for privacy during this difficult time. In lieu of flowers, donations may be made to fortify the Arch Cape Animal Shelter.

Fin closed the browser tab. *That's enough wheel-spinning for one day. Enough for a lifetime.*

FIN GOT TAKEOUT from a local Thai place and watched the sun dip past the horizon from her rental's deck. The days were starting to feel the same. Wake up, breakfast, work, read. Then walk, lunch, research, obsess. Dinner, check in with Marnie, read, wine, and explore Mom's journal, which was face down on the living room coffee table.

Get sad and drink too much to cope. Wish that things were different.

After her meal, she went inside with the remains of her chicken curry and tossed the takeout carton in the refrigerator. A bottle of imported Cabernet Franc waited on the counter. She creaked it open and found that she had to wash a wine glass—she'd run out of the four provided in record time—before pouring her first glass of the night. Was she becoming an alcoholic? Whatever, it wasn't like she drank this much at home. Fin took her glass and went to her usual place in the living room: the cozy couch. *I'll drink much less in LA*, Fin told herself. She grabbed the diary from its home on the coffee table and sat back—found her place at the end of the April thirteenth entry.

How dare I leave him for cheating on me all those times? How dare I want a better life?

I'm not perfect. I make plenty of mistakes like everyone else, but Christ. And then one of those mistakes sauntered in and made a bigger mess.

Harrison was already drunk when he arrived at the party, like last time at Musso & Frank. He noticed Theo, then saw Roy (who gave him a look that read not to fuck with him, hee-hee), and then promptly picked a fight with Theo. Even more hilarious, Harrison actually called Theo a slut! He said, "Hey, how's my favorite man-slut?" I tried so hard not to laugh, but it was impossible. Roy and I snorted. They heard us, and both of them shot us looks that could kill. Whatever. Guys are so territorial and weird, even when they don't want you. Or do they? Somehow, most of them are never not-exhausting. Roy is such a refreshing exception to these high school shenanigans.

Theo then took advantage of Harrison's weakened state, asking when the last time he'd showered had been. Then he asked the crowd, "Which bitch invited this louse?" Then

Harrison asked pretty loudly which brothel Theo's date was from! Holy shit, what behavior. I have to admit that it was hysterical, however. Comedic relief from the rest of the drama.

Theo detached himself from the girl and went up to Harrison, who'd sauntered to the pool bar for another libation. He jabbed him in the shoulder and threatened, "Get lost, loser. You're not welcome here."

"Or what?" Harrison bellowed, and tossed his fresh drink in Theo's face.

That alcohol must have stung his eyes. Or his pride was badly hurt. Or a fun blend of the two, because then Theo punched Harrison hard in the gut.

When he doubled over, Theo grabbed him rough by the shoulders. He whispered what looked like something menacing in Harrison's ears—his face went white—and he looked at me.

It's hard to describe what was in Harrison's eyes as he stared… Maybe pity mixed with terror? I have no idea what Theo said to him, but I got a really bad feeling from that look.

It only lasted a second before Theo tossed him in the pool. "Cool down, you drunk fuck!" It was like a goddamn movie. Everyone stared.

Things weren't so funny anymore. Roy turned and looked at me as if trying to comprehend such barbaric behavior. It was embarrassing. All I could do was shrug and sip my mimosa. Nothing felt real.

Harrison slithered out of the pool and coughed out some water. He was fully dressed when Theo had thrown him in. He sat on the edge of the pool for a few minutes, deciding what to do. It was sad and pathetic.

Eventually, he came over to us, some kind of shell-shocked look on his face, water squelching out of his shoes. He pulled a soggy doll from his pocket, put it on the table, and wished

Finley a happy birthday while laying a big, wet kiss on me. I turned my face in time so that the kiss landed on my cheek, not my mouth.

Roy watched, silent, ready to belt him into next week if needed, I think. But Harrison ambled off and left without any more commotion, which was for the best.

As he was leaving, Theo shouted at Harrison's back that he better never touch me or Finley again.

Does he want us back? He was being protective of his daughter and ex-wife, I suppose… But the way he yelled, it felt like he was saying he owned us. He certainly does not. If he wanted to keep us, he should have treated us better. Tough shit!

Worse—I got chills at the way he barked while shooting daggers at me with his eyes.

Roy didn't say much, but he saw it. He observed everything. Maybe he was trying to assess what he'd gotten himself into. I hope this madness doesn't drive him away.

He was even kinder to me than usual, however. I'm grateful for that.

Theo stuck around, as if to prove a point or something. I avoided him as much as I could, and I tossed that soggy doll in the trash on the way out.

April 15, 1979

We don't have a ton of time to spend together off set, but every minute with Roy fills me with happiness and hope. I'd love to take a trip with him somewhere after wrap. I hear Puerto Vallarta's nice, but I'd go anywhere with Roy.

I really like this guy.

But I know this is Hollywood, so maybe he's like this with every co-star on every production. He might just forget about me when he's paired with the next pretty actress. Temptation is a huge reason for Hollywood relationships not working out. I'm guilty of it myself.

I'm trying not to hope too much, but when I'm not with Roy, I think about him. There's a look in his eyes sometimes that leads me to believe he feels similarly. But…does he want a kid? This is such a hard industry on love and family. Just look at my current situation—I've got an actor ex-husband who couldn't keep it in his pants, and I follow that by getting too close to my manager, also an ex-actor.

Now I may be falling in love with another actor. I know what we can be like. Why do I do this to myself? Fucking actors, man.

If only… Ugh, it's no use dreaming about other lives and what could be if we met under different circumstances. At the same time, I love my life. Especially when I think about what else I could have become. Imagine me working as a secretary or a bank teller somewhere. So boring.

And no one would remember me after I'm gone.

"Not true, Mom," Fin murmured.

We can't change what we are. Best to try and be happy, and do good work.

April 17, 1979

I had an incredible time with Roy tonight. I just wrapped! The production still has another week, but I'm free for a little bit now. We'll see if they need me for pick-ups, but the director really seems to know what he's doing, so I doubt it. This is one of those films that I can just tell is going to be good, if not great.

Roy took me to dinner since we finished up around 7 p.m., which is always nice. I'm glad my last day wasn't a night shoot. Those are hard on everyone. Anyway, this gentleman has blown everyone else I've ever been with away, by far. I know I keep writing about it, but I'm infatuated. Maybe his manners and good charm have something to do with the fact that he wasn't raised in America.

No, he's charmingly British (with a touch of Welsh and French), and to my surprise, tans well. That's good, since he's playing a southerner from Texas on this project, ha-ha. Roy's been classically trained, too, and has done a ton of theater in London. The director actually found him on Broadway in a supporting role and had to fight to get him cast—he's never been in an American film before—so it was an uphill battle from the start. But Roy's screen test was apparently a knockout, and from there on, it's been smooth sailing for him.

Honestly, he should have been the lead in this picture. I think he can be more well-known on this continent. I can't imagine Roy will have any trouble booking the lead in the next film, though. He and our director get on well, and I think they'll both have sterling careers.

I just hope they don't forget about me.

Look at me, all lovelorn.

Whatever will be, will be.

Roy also gave me a beautiful wrap-gift, just because. It's a lush, rabbit-fur jacket, with so many colors in it. I love it.

"For cold nights," he said. "I saw it window shopping and knew you had to have it. I hope I guessed the right size."

Oh my GOD. He was so bashful!

I tried it on, and it fit perfectly.

He kissed my hand and nuzzled his face on the fur sleeve. Ahhhh! Who does this? It might have been creepy if anyone else had done this, but from him, it felt like an act of love.

Which we made a lot of that night. I feel so safe.

In bed, Roy held me and said he wants nothing more than to keep seeing me. I had to bite back the words, "I love you," but I let my eyes do the talking. I need him to be the one to say it first. I'm afraid I'll scare him away.

Do the British raise their own to be so seductive, so protective? I think the world should know, if so.

He's special. Movie-star special. Melt-your-heart special. I have really good feelings about what's next for us, both in our professional trajectory and our love lives.

We've made plans to attend the premiere of Running to the Sea *together. I don't know what I'll wear or when that will be, but I can't wait. It's going to feel incredible to wear something completely unaffordable just for the night. And I get to be on his arm! The studio's publicist said she can recommend some designers when the time comes. And I just know that Roy will shine in a tux.*

I might die right there on the red carpet, we'll see.

But, does Roy mean what he says? I would give anything for this thing between us to last. I need this relationship to be real.

I keep going over the dates we've had, as well as our chemistry, both on and off camera. I don't think he's full of shit, he really seems sincere. Every time he speaks, I forget myself. It's like we're the only ones in the room, or the only people alive. Close up, gentle light, soft focus.

I'm going to hang onto the impossible—and to him—for as long as I can.

"Wow," Fin breathed. She wiped at the moisture in her eyes and tried not to think of what her life could have been. She gave herself ten minutes on the deck, in the cold sea air, to reset herself before continuing.

April 19, 1979

I finally found the courage to break it off with Harrison for good yesterday. It was hard and scary. Let's face it, these things are always excruciating. But I did it in broad daylight in Santa Monica, down on the pier, with tons of people around.

I felt relieved that he didn't make much of a scene. Harrison even said that he understood. However, he did look like a puppy who'd been kicked in the face, and that was awful. He already seemed sad when we met that day, but with a weird kind of nervous energy. Even after this, he asked if we could still continue working together.

I'm not sure that's such a good idea. I said maybe, to try and placate him. He falls prey to fits of jealousy and anger, and I don't feel like being an emotional punching bag anymore. I sure as hell don't want to be tied to him the way I am to Theo.

Then he surprised me by asking if we could "escape together" for a weekend, to workshop a script he's written. It's his first script. He just finished it, and he wants me to star in the project.

Fin cringed. She wanted to yell, "Don't do it!" But this was the past. Harrison—or someone else—had interfered. The timeline in the diary tracked. Mom had disappeared shortly after these entries were written.

Fin refilled her glass and practically inhaled half of it. She wasn't looking forward to whatever she might read next. It was fairly obvious how this was going to end. There wasn't much left to go. *Let's get this over with.*

Harrison says he's got some financiers interested and that he may produce it himself. He even started to throw around crew ideas. He likes the director I'm working with now, but the director doesn't like him, so good luck, pal.

I want to be kind and help him out…but this is not in my best interest. However, I feel guilty about how things have worked out. I've jumped from one man to another, and now, yet another (even though he's amazing).

But what would Roy think of this, me going away for the weekend with a recent ex? This is so early on in our relationship that it's either fine, and we're both free to do what we like, or…

I ruin everything. I never get to hear that delightful accent calling me "Merry" ever again. That purr in my ear, Jesus, what it does to me. I don't get to feel Roy's intimate caresses, or his lips and teeth nipping at the sensitive spot on my neck anymore. I destroy a chance at the best relationship I've ever had, because a man has coerced me into something that I don't want to do.

Story of every woman's life.

I told him that I'll think about it, which I'm doing now. If I help Harrison, will this put him on a different track? I'd love for him to focus on this project and not on me. I don't know. Maybe I can just give him notes and that'll be the end of it.

I don't think I'll go. I'll see if I can think of any other actresses that would like this opportunity—no, wait, I can't willingly do that to anyone.

No, I have to make a clean break.

I can't take responsibility for him, for his feelings, for the damage he's done to his own career. Let him fail. Let him discover what it means to be the only one who's been burning down his life. I wonder if he's capable of such self-reflection.

But you know what? I don't have to worry about that, anymore, do I?

"No, you do not," Fin agreed, and turned the page.

May 1, 1979

I met Harrison at a café today. Stupid, I know. I wore extra-heavy eyeshadow and liner. War paint.

I'd been putting it off since the script was delivered by courier a week ago. Yesterday, I read the script over the course of a bath. Or skimmed it, rather.

He tortures the lead character in it, the role I'd play. I wonder if what he writes are the things he wants to do to me.

I told him no about the weekend getaway and everything else. I didn't try to sugarcoat it, and I'm proud of myself for that. I just said it wasn't in my best interest and I wished him luck on the project. I also told him that I'm seeking new representation.

He didn't like any of that, but who cares? I need to do what's right for me, my daughter, and our future. Finley deserves better, as do her children, should she ever have any. I have to think more about being a good role model and what kind of environment I create.

I have to focus on the light, not the darkness.

It was not lost on Fin how similar her situation was to her mother's, decades ago.

May 2, 1979

I found a dead rat on my doorstep.
It could have died there naturally.
I have a feeling it did not.

Fin gasped at the last sentence, ice shooting through her veins.

She turned the page—blank. The rest of the diary was empty.

Fin closed the book with a soft respect. She let it rest on her lap. This was the end of a life.

She didn't know how else to chase away the horrific finality of that. So, she shut herself off, turned on the television, and nursed her glass of wine.

DARKNESS.

The sound of an old phone line trying to connect—*click, click, pop, click.*

A cryptic warning:

"She wants to control you. He'll find you out. Leave before you can't."

ACT 3

THURSDAY

"WAKE UP."

Fin shifted, lids parting open. She'd fallen asleep on the couch, aided by the wine and the area's endless, low-pressure weather. Voices called; the TV was on. Actors confronted each other over secrets. Words were had. The quiet shouting across the room wasn't enough to make her care about being awake. She pulled the handcrafted blanket up and around her shoulders and settled deeper into the cushions. Sleep crept up her limbs, but a female voice pierced through her drowsy cocoon.

"I'm talking to you, Finley," came the reprimand.

Now she was wide awake, her brain screaming, mouth dry.

This is not possible.

Her mother stared at her from the flat-screen television, one of the few modern touches in the rental home. This had to be one of her mother's old films, and Fin had heard wrong while slipping in and out of dreamland.

But the shot on the TV didn't switch to another actor. The camera stayed in a close-up, trained on Meredith

Lyon's pale face, framed by fiery red ringlets. Her icy blue eyes were locked on Fin.

Is this the past? Is this now?

Now in a new scene, her mom turned and plucked a few flowers from a bush, admired the beauty of the pale pink roses. She appeared to be the same age she was when she'd disappeared, right after she'd wrapped on *Running to the Sea*.

This was that movie! Fin had seen the film many times before. It was one of Mom's best. No, *the* best. Her supporting role was a meaty one, infused with weariness and passion, not unlike Elizabeth Taylor's stranger characters. The film took on a deeper significance now that Fin had digested the journal entries, now that she knew more about the events surrounding the film.

The scene dissolved to a close up of a pen on paper, writing in a journal. Another dissolve on screen resulted in a tsunami of weakness that threatened to overtake Fin, the room shifting before her. She swayed and gripped the couch cushions beneath her, digging her nails into the fabric, hoping to anchor herself.

Did I drink too much? Please, make this stop.

She inhaled. *1, 2, 3, 4, 5, 6...* Counted until she felt her mind calming. The movie was still playing when she opened her eyes.

What do I know about this film, inexplicably playing for me? What can I learn if I can push aside fear?

Running to the Sea hadn't been an ordinary drama for the time. It centered on the lives of two couples who'd become too interchangeable with themselves. They'd become so tangled in one another's lives that they all started to unravel, fighting and sleeping together. Alliances would fray and strengthen as the story ebbed and flowed.

Fin thought she felt a featherweight touch on the back of her neck. *Oh-god, oh-god.* She huffed and hugged herself, squeezed her eyes tighter. *Concentrate!*

This train-wreck of on-screen relationships—as dramatic as those Meredith had with Theo, Harrison, and Roy in real life—had been too intense for most mainstream audiences when it was released in late 1979. Mixed critical reviews were the norm, as a result. From what Fin had read, some critics had panned it as a degradation of the American nucleus of romantic partnerships and the family. Others had shouted that for this very reason, the film should have had more Academy Award nominations than it did—particularly for acting, direction, and the acerbic script. Roy had been nominated for Best Supporting Actor, and the film was nominated for Best Score.

Some of those reviews had called out Mom's performance, one even going so far as to liken it to a simmering tea kettle before boiling. What that really meant was that Meredith's restraint in keeping her character's anger just below the surface while committing emotional subterfuge (she'd been the villainous architect of the group's disharmony) was masterful.

Many reviews commented on the chemistry she'd had with Roy, how perfectly they played off one another.

I wish you had lived so much longer. I wish you had both been my parents.

Others had said that the diminutive actress's presence was uncanny, but they'd had difficulty determining exactly why. Something about her had been unsettling to these mostly male reviewers. It was as if they thought Meredith had access to some secret, pagan realm, by the way she carried herself. A place inhabited by powerful, frightening witches—a protected territory to which their overt maleness could never grant them access. They revered her, but also feared her. It was obvious to anyone who read their film reviews and the way they wrote about her.

The scene changed again. It started with a slow pan across the shoreline to Roy's character, who sat shirtless, dusting sand off his palms. Mom watched as the tanned Brit turned over on the beach blanket they shared. He grinned at her before settling face down for a sunny nap.

In the next shot, Mom dragged her fingers through the sand, creating a lazy trail. She scooped up a palm full of the stuff and turned her hand over, letting the sand go in the breeze. As if her palm was an hourglass.

Time's running out.

Meredith's character stopped what she was doing and looked through the television to her daughter.

Shit. Fin closed her eyes, trying desperately to quell the panic rising in her. She dug her nails into her palms and concentrated on the history surrounding the movie.

In most cases, reviews held the general consensus that if Mom hadn't disappeared, her career would have skyrocketed, perhaps even to legendary status. From watching *Running to the Sea*, it was easy to see why. Fin had no doubt that Mom's own troubles with visions beyond the veil had informed her performances.

Roy and the other co-stars had gone on to great acclaim.

Fin made a mental note to look him up online, now that she knew what he'd meant to her mother. She could enlist Aunt Mary's help. *Was he still alive? What about the other cast members? She could look them up too. It was possible that one of them knew something that could help her.*

Like Fin's imagination, Hollywood gossip had birthed many theories and rumors, but none were ever proved correct. In the end, the actress had become another haunting casualty of the entertainment industry. The beautiful and talented Meredith Lyons had joined the ranks of the doomed ghosts from which Hollywood paved its streets. A town where every new opportunity comes from stepping over the dead.

Fin opened her eyes again. Mom wasn't finished with her. This illusion—*delusion, haunting, mental illness, phantasm*—would not stop until Mom was ready for it to stop.

"What's going on?" Fin asked.

"You're in the right place," Mom said, and the television picture glitched. Rainbow pixels danced apart in waves and then pulled themselves back together to again create the image of her mother. She had a pointed look on her face—determined. *Ruthless.*

Fin opened her mouth to speak again, to question the dead, but the screen winked out. Black.

The only ghosts left were her own.

OVERCAST DAYLIGHT FLOODED her vision as she opened her eyes. *Was I asleep? I must have been. It's becoming harder and harder to tell what's real.*

Something jabbed into her side, and she sat up to discover that she'd been sleeping on the remote. A dream, then. It was likely that she'd been half awake and rolled over on it, which accounted for the television shutting off.

Fin sat up and checked the time on her phone.

Ten missed calls from Marnie, including a voicemail. *Shit.*

The voicemail was chilling and brief. First, Marnie's voice rang out, plaintive and desperate: "Mommy!!!" Then, Mary's voice could be hear in the background, attempting to soothe the girl. Then the message ended.

Fin checked the time of the calls against the current time on her phone. Only an hour had passed. She called Marnie back, and on the second ring, she heard her child's voice.

"Mommy."

"Baby," she answered. "I just got your message. What happened? Is Auntie with you?"

"Yeah." The small voice sighed. "Just a minute."

Fin listened to the soft, rustling sounds of footsteps, followed by the sound of the bedroom door closing. "Good job, Marnie. Privacy's important for us."

"I know, Mom. I'm okay now. I told Auntie I had a nightmare."

Fin knew it was not a nightmare. It was reality. Marnie would forever have to watch mold sprout and grow on the faces of others, and on her own face when reflected. It was the price she'd have to pay to stay out of the reach of invasive doctors and psychiatrists. It fucking killed Fin that her daughter would have to endure this for the rest of her life. *Sorry, kid.*

"Was it Mrs. Don't again?"

"Daddy," Marnie said.

A shock ran up Fin's spine. "What?"

"I saw Daddy. He didn't look okay." Marnie started to cry. "He was hurt." *Oh, God.* Marnie continued to mewl in the saddest way Fin had ever heard. "Where is he, Mommy?"

I never wanted this. If only things could have been different. Tears welled up, then spilled down her cheeks. "I don't know, honey. I wish I did. I'm sorry."

Fin stood and caught her reflection in a mirror framed by seashells on the opposite wall.

It couldn't be. It was impossible.

Black, oily bubbles rose and imploded over where her eyes were supposed to be.

She almost screamed.

For Marnie's sake, Fin sat down on the couch, where she could remain calm. She grabbed the diary from the table. *Blue. Find more blue things.* She found three shades of blue in the knotted rug by the door. Through the doorway to the kitchen, the robin's-egg blue tea kettle was perched on the stove top. The modal cotton lounge set she wore was navy blue with tiny stars.

"Mommy?"

Marnie's voice was a rock, unmovable in a storm.

"Yes, baby."

"When are you coming home?"

What the fuck day is it? Thursday. Tomorrow morning is check-out.

"Um, I'm leaving tomorrow, and I'll be home sometime on Saturday" she answered. She didn't want to promise anything. "I love you, Marnie."

"I love you too, Mommy."

"Hey, what do you think about going to Disneyland this weekend? Just you and me? Would that be fun?"

"Yeah!" Marnie chirped. Her sudden joy felt to Fin like the sun bursting through heavy clouds.

Kids are resilient. She'll be okay.

"You got it, baby. I'm gonna go pack now so I can leave bright and early in the morning. Okay?"

"Okay! Drive safe, Mom! I love you!"

The call ended before Fin could say goodbye. At least she'd given Marnie something to look forward to, whether she could afford it or not.

What the fuck happened to my eyes when I told her that I didn't know where Jeff was? Nothing made sense. She stood again and went to the mirror. The terrible, tar-like bubbles were gone. *I don't get it. I wasn't lying!*

A split-second later, a small sphere appeared and burst on her forehead.

What the fuck!!

Enough mirrors. She returned to the coffee table strewn with books, her laptop, and an empty wine bottle. Last night's glass sat on her mom's old lobby card for *Running to the Sea*. The photo paper's emulsion had cracked in the center, splitting her mother from Roy.

How different life would be, with a love like that.

Fin grabbed the bottle, glass, and her laptop, and headed to the kitchen. She could make the last of the eggs she'd bought from Arch General for breakfast and boil some tea. While she waited for the eggs to cook, she sat down at the kitchen table with her laptop and typed "Roy Treadwell" into the web browser's search bar.

Some video results came up, including his acceptance speech for the 1980 Academy Awards. *Wow.* The thumbnail showed the very handsome man in a tuxedo, leaning over the microphone, holding his golden statue.

She clicked on the video. It started with a title card for "Best Supporting Actor." Next, the camera cut between the male nominees that were awaiting their fate. Fin recognized the woman sitting with Roy. She'd been the lead actress in *Running to the Sea*. The male lead was seated on her other side.

A pair of pretty people, a gorgeous actress and a devilish actor, stood at the podium. They clapped and waited for the audience applause to die down. The actress opened the seal on a thick, glossy envelope and smiled, her mouth full of white teeth, her lips a dark crimson. "And the Best Supporting Actor Award goes to… Roy Treadwell!"

The theater erupted in applause, and the camera fell on Roy, who'd been sitting in a pensive way, hands tented together beneath his chin. His co-stars congratulated him, kissing and hugging, slapping each other on the back. But Roy wasn't nearly as cheerful as they were.

To Fin, it looked like he was trying to hold back tears as he accepted the accolades. A deep sadness was buried beneath his tight smile, showed through in the way he held himself. It was the stiff politeness one wears when trying to hold emotions together in a public setting.

I know what that's like.

In this little window to the past, Fin watched him walk to the stage. The glamorous actress-presenter kissed him on the cheek, and the actor gave him a one-armed hug and clap on the back. Roy barely noticed they were there. He took the Oscar, turned it over a few times in his hand, weighed its heaviness in his grip. The applause died down, and with hesitation, he addressed his peers.

"This is a bit of a miracle, I think. Are you sure you've got the right person?" Roy smiled at the resulting chuckles, but his eyes didn't match the grin. "I thank the Academy, our mighty director James, our stalwart producer Steven, my family at the Royal Academy of Dramatic Arts back home, my agent Walt, and my wonderful co-stars, Richard and Sandy." Roy waited for the polite applause to die down before continuing. He looked down at the podium and swallowed back his emotion. Ever the performer, he tried a brighter smile before looking back at the well-heeled crowd.

You still look so unbearably sad, Fin thought. *I can feel it decades later.*

"But I have yet to say a few words about my favorite partner on this film. Yes, I'm biased. She was—*is*—a terrific actress and human being: Meredith Lyons." The room fell to a somber hush, and Roy's smile faded. His eyes looked haunted. *Was that guilt?* He recovered quickly and blinked back his vulnerability. "*Merry*, I called her. She was one of a kind—generous, hilarious, talented, spunky, and taken from us much too soon. We don't know what happened, Merry, but you should be with us here, celebrating—"

The hurry-the-fuck-up music started playing, which caused Roy to stop and look stage-right. He was noticeably uncomfortable.

Fin frowned. *Fuck you, Hollywood.*

"I hope you're still out there, Merry—somehow, somewhere. We miss you. Thank you."

The exit music swelled, too bright and brassy. Roy took a last look at his audience. Fin tried to sense what he might have felt in that moment. If it had been her on that stage, she'd have a hard time even being there at all, no less accepting the industry's highest award while having lost her love in a tragic way—all in public, all while pretending to keep it together. Roy sighed and marched offstage. The music was an insult. Fin wondered if Roy had walked straight to his car after the acceptance speech. She would have.

The tea kettle whistled. Fin grabbed the kettle from the stove and poured the steaming water over a bag of chai. *Was Roy still alive?*

A quick search revealed that he was still very much alive and working in the United Kingdom. He'd done dozens of films and television shows since winning the Oscar, including two more films with James, the director of *Running to the Sea.*

Fin added the word "contact" to her internet search and hit the enter key.

There it was: thanks to the magic of the twenty-first century, Roy Treadwell's U.K. film and television agency appeared, complete with mailing address and phone number. She clicked on his personal info and found a recent head shot, along with his resume. At the bottom of the page was a link that read, "Inquire." *How politely British.*

Could she really write to this guy's agency and say, *"Hey, I don't have a script for you to consider, but I'm the daughter of an actress you dated decades ago? I'd love to ask you some questions about her disappearance."*

She took the tea bag out of her mug and replaced it with a splash of almond milk.

Fuck it. Fin clicked the link to inquire.

FIN IMMEDIATELY REGRETTED writing to Roy. It was unlikely that his agency would forward the message. They probably received strange emails every day. Even if they took her email seriously, she would be their lowest priority. It wasn't like she was a producer with an offer.

Still, the way Meredith had written about Roy… He'd have a hard time forgetting that kind of love. *Wouldn't he?*

Fin decided on a shower to pass the time, so she plodded to the bathroom and turned on the water. She was about to get undressed when the air around her started feeling ticklish, like invisible wisps of hair were brushing along her skin. She didn't feel quite right, like the part of her that identified as Fin hit a snag and was being pulled outside of herself. Her body was a garment, and she was the thread coming undone.

Is this a heart attack? Am I dying? Fin had never felt anything like this.

And that's when she felt something move into her body and replace her.

The bathroom mirror showed the same pale face, blue eyes, and straight red hair that had been reflected back at Fin her entire life, but something about the image was different. *Wrong.*

Something else was gazing back at her through her own freaking eyes.

She tried to scream, but a knot formed in her throat. Fin gripped the sink with white knuckles and dry-heaved.

The reflection—it's me, but not me.

Sweat trickled from her hairline and down her face. Her skin felt flushed, but she never looked more pale in her life. It felt like the worst fever imaginable. Death was coming for her. She started to hyperventilate.

"You're okay," she said to her reflection.

But that wasn't true. And Fin's voice wasn't hers. She lifted a trembling hand to her neck, touched where she imagined her larynx to be. She knew this strange voice well, but only from past recordings.

"You're okay," Fin said again, but like before, it was her mother's voice being spoken from her lips.

"What's happening?!" Her voice was still not her own.

"You'll see soon enough," Mom said.

Fin choked. *"Please don't,"* she begged.

Her vision spun like she was falling from the sky.

BLURRY WHITE CEILING tiles, skin warm and moist, hard floor beneath her. Fin was lying on her back. She turned her head and tried not to wretch. Hot water was still pouring from the showerhead. She latched onto the sound of the running water and let it steady her.

I'm okay. I'm safe. I don't think I'm too hurt.

She wondered how long ago she'd been down. A dull pain pulsed in her forehead. As she straightened, she recoiled at the touch of vomit on the bath rug. She searched her scalp for injuries but found none.

I feel sick. I don't know if I can drive home tomorrow. What's happening to me??

Fin wasn't sure what else to do but crawl into the tub and let the water rain down on her, so she did. If she was lucky, the hot stream against her skin would set her free from whatever had taken her from herself.

THE SHOWER HAD helped. So had the blueberry scone from Arch General, which she nibbled at like a mouse and washed down with more tea.

But even after all that, she still couldn't shake the feeling that someone else was here with her, inside her, *wearing* her like a skin-suit. The sensation was heavy, and it slowed her down, kept her in a fog, felt like she had slugged an entire bottle of cold medicine and was now a mindless zombie.

Something inside her longed for fresh sea air. It was a desire she couldn't explain.

A walk then.

BUNDLED UP AND snug in her winter coat and beanie, Fin walked along the beach. The blustery sea air was welcome against her face. She found herself waking, her senses sharpened by the cold. The nausea, too, had begun to fade. She inhaled a long pull of sea air—*ah, the medicinal powers of sea salt*—and tried to distract herself with the windblown scenery. The encroaching shoreline told her that the tide would be rolling in soon.

After another few minutes of walking, a cave appeared. The caves around her were a favorite of travel bloggers and social media influencers alike, but despite having visited this area many times before, Fin had never taken the opportunity to explore them herself. She looked again to the rising tide and then trekked into the cave.

The cave amplified the roar of the waves outside like a giant conch shell held to one's ear. Despite her troubles, a smile formed on Fin's lips. It was like she were a child again. Curious. Resilient.

A red glow emanated from the back of the cave, and the sight made Fin feel weak. Her vision started to grow dark. *No, no, no! If you pass out here, you'll drown! Is this what happened to Mom?* She slapped one cheek and then the other to shock her system awake. She stomped her feet in a second effort to help wake her body up.

The red glow brightened until that terrible sense of being watched returned.

The light wants me to come to it. It won't hurt me. I don't think.

She sucked in a sharp mouthful of air and approached the light. It pulsed, getting brighter as she closed in on it. Beneath the rugged crook of rock wall, something partially buried there shimmered.

Fin scraped at the sand floor with her nails and pulled out a small, metallic object. It was a filigree garnet ring.

I know this ring. This belonged to Mom.

The tide swirled around her boots. She'd either lost time again or miscalculated it terribly. Either way, cold water engulfed her ankles. She turned and ran, fighting against the incoming tide. She had to escape back to the beach before the current got too strong and buried her right here in this cave—just like it might have done to her mother.

RATTLED, FIN ESCAPED the cave and rushed back to the cottage, where she locked and bolted the door. She fetched the worn binder that contained the evidence of her mother's life and flipped to a particular page. The headline there read, "Rising Star Missing." Fin's eyes dropped to the more startling subhead: "Actress Meredith Lyons Feared Dead."

"Mom," Fin breathed.

Meredith's final head shot accompanied the story in all her retro, free-spirited beauty, a hand coyly entwined in her curls.

A filigree garnet ring curved around one of those graceful fingers—the very same one Fin now held in her hand.

Another twinge inside her. She blinked. That same terrible snag pulled at her again. She hated the loss of control. She doubled over, then jerked up, her eyelids fluttering like dying butterflies.

A compulsive desire to wear the ring came over her. *NO!* A flicker of panic lit in her belly but was extinguished faster than it had started, like someone had doused the tiny flame with purpose. Fin no longer felt in control, as if she had been brushed aside completely.

I'm not driving anymore. I'm a passenger.

Her body filled with an odd, inappropriate sense of calm.

But there's peace in letting someone else take the wheel.

She slipped the silver ring over a finger, like it was made just for her.

The color of the ring's stone intensified, glowing from garnet to radiant ruby. It was as if the gem was lit from within, growing more luminous and powerful. It fortified her.

She turned her head and sniffed. *Foul.* A presence was near. Not a nice one, either. Not like he portrayed himself to be.

You FUCK.

Fin stood as if pulled upright by an invisible string, the binder falling from her lap and crashing to the floor with a clatter. Her head swiveled to the window. She jangled around inside herself while someone else piloted, her limbs off-balance and flailing. She stumbled to the window and snatched a curtain out of the way.

Once again, Charlie was walking Moxie outside.

"Harrison Bentley," Fin growled, but it was the voice and thoughts of her mother.

Together, they watched Charlie stroll down the street with his dog, not a goddamn care in the world.

We'll see about that.

BACK OUTSIDE, FIN surveyed the neighborhood with a detached sense of recognition. The sleepy seaside village held no threat; there were barely any people in the area. Only locals were still around, and some of them were gone on vacation in warmer climates.

Fin trailed Charlie, keeping far enough behind him to stay out of Moxie's detection range.

The heat of rage engulfed her. It warmed her so much that she unzipped her coat and let it flap open as she pursued. The cool breeze was quite welcome against her burning skin. A smirk pulled at the corner of her mouth.

One of us is going to die today, and it won't be me.

Jesus! These thoughts aren't mine.

Take a back seat, Finley. Momma's driving now.

Fin ripped off her beanie and shoved it in her pocket. Had she finally cracked enough for a lifelong trip to a mental institution? Or would Jeff take custody of Marnie and have Fin thrown out onto the street?

It'd be more efficient to kill myself!

Stop talking like that, my love. Just watch. You'll see.

In the distance, Harrison climbed a hill near a small waterfall.

Fin tried to shake off whatever madness had claimed her, but to no avail. She followed the old man up the hill.

The closer she got, the more feverish she felt. Every step was a mile.

Fin stopped when Charlie and Moxie reached the edge of the tree line—and the cliff.

I could run and kick him over the edge. He deserves it.

Had Charlie really done something so bad that he deserved to die? And if so, what?

Time to end this.

I don't want to kill an old man. I don't want to kill anyone!

Fin struggled to get the reins back, kicking within her. She felt herself being pulled to the ground, out of breath as if her lungs had collapsed. She panted and gasped. Her body rumbled, shaking like the start of a controlled detonation.

Something is very wrong with me, and I don't know if I can survive this.

Fin fell to her knees. Her vision went in and out of focus, and she heard herself grunt and groan, struggling for control of her mind. But this inner battle only further infuriated the spirit of her mother and intensified her drive.

In the distance, Charlie pivoted. He spotted Fin, and his face contorted in confusion.

A strangled roar escaped Fin's lips, foam seeping out of the corners of her mouth, and then everything went black.

DARKNESS.

Trees branches swayed in the sky above her. Shadows faded in and out.

Help. God. Where am I…?

She felt the sensation of being dragged, as if on a sled, across rocky land, heard the sound of pebbles scraping and scratching beneath. Her vision bounced. A world out of focus.

Then back into the void.

"THERE, THERE," THE voice said. It was warm and grandfatherly.

A cool, damp cloth moved across Fin's forehead, wiping the delirium from her face. She attempted to open her eyes.

"Finley!" Charlie exclaimed. His face peered over hers with deep concern. "You're still with us. My God, I just about had a heart attack watching you go down like that on the rocks. Are you okay? Do you need a hospital?"

Fin moaned and looked around from her place on the couch. *Mom?* Somehow, Charlie had gotten Fin back into the cottage. She saw the coffee table and her things. The old binder still laid face down on the floor.

Charlie offered a glass to her. "Water?"

She nodded, her throat made of sandpaper. Charlie helped her sit up enough to take a sip. The drink was such a sudden relief, like a fire extinguisher putting out an inferno. Fin snatched the glass and swallowed it all, greedy and needful. Water streamed out of both sides of her mouth in trickles as she gulped.

"Whoa," Charlie murmured. "Should I get more?"

Am I okay? Will I puke? Nodding again, Fin tested herself to see if it was all right to fully sit up. She was shaky but strong enough. Her head hurt, and she rubbed the dull ache at her brow.

Charlie stood, empty glass in hand. "Well, kiddo, the good thing is that I don't think we need an ambulance. But you look like you could use some Aspirin. How about it?"

"Yeah," was all she could eke out. "Sounds great."

He lumbered off somewhere—to the medicine cabinet in the bathroom, most likely.

Her eyes fell to the binder splayed on the floor.

Fin leaned over, careful of her equilibrium. *I feel like a shaken snow globe.* She watched the entrance of the hallway where Charlie had disappeared. She couldn't allow him to see her and become suspicious of the binder's content. She was weak but willed herself forward.

Almost there. A little bit farther now.

"You scared the hell out of me," Charlie's voice called.

She jerked at the sound of his voice. Her fingers grasped for the edge of the plastic binder and she pulled it close. She snapped the binder shut and slipped it back into her bag on the floor, then shoved the bag aside with her foot.

Charlie came back into the living room and walked over to Fin with a full glass of water and two white pills. Normally, she'd never take either from a man she didn't know, but these were extraordinary circumstances.

"Thanks," Fin croaked, choking down the medicine with a gulp of water. She emptied the glass for a second time and looked into his watery blue eyes. Something about him unsettled her. She wanted to shriek, maybe vomit. Or shriek while vomiting. Both felt appropriate.

Rather, she dug her nails into her palms and squeaked, "Sorry. I don't know what's come over me. I'm really not feeling like myself right now." Fin offered a faint smile… and giggled.

A nagging thought—something needing to be freed—and then she was being piloted by someone else again. *Goddammit!*

Fin listened as her voice took on a coquettish lilt. "Charlie… Have you been lifting weights? How'd you get me all the way back here?"

The man seemed at a loss for words but quickly recovered with a chuckle. *Peacocking.* "Oh, I guess I'm stronger than I look," he said, taking on the rakish favor of his youth. "I like to keep active—run, lift weights."

A black bubble formed on his cheek, and when it popped, it spit viscous black goo.

"I'm ever so grateful," Fin purred, not in Fin's voice. She brushed a lock of hair out of her eye with the hand that wore Meredith's ring. She imagined it throwing off light to catch Charlie's eye, glowing on its own accord, as it had in the cave.

He saw it, and recognition flickered in his eyes. He took an involuntary step back, and his mouth dropped open, all traces of his bravado gone.

What kind of short circuiting is happening in his brain right now? A fine blend of confusion, doubt, and terror, I hope. She smiled wider.

"Well, I should leave you to rest," he murmured, shuffling away.

That's right. Shit your pants.

Charlie opened the door and stopped, and when he turned back around, he was somehow whiter than usual. "Did you say something?"

Did I?

"Hmm?" Fin asked.

They stared at each other. He looked afraid. *Good.*

A muscle in her neck contracted to tilt her head to the side, then another in her face moved her lips, formed them into garish smile, cartoonish and fake. *I'm in the back seat again. Mom's going to drive us straight off a cliff.*

"Thank you so much for taking such good care of me, *Charlie.*" His eyes widened, and she continued. "You're truly a good man. I don't know what I would've done without you," Meredith's words dripped with honey.

The silence between them was a gulf.

"No problem," he finally said. "Glad to help. Call if you need me."

"I sure will, handsome," Mom said, and blew him a kiss.

They watched him leave, eyes following him out the door. He slammed it shut, spooked.

They rose and went to a window, through which they peered at him. He stopped, and their eyes connected. She smiled and waved, sending him hotfooting it back home.

FIN'S MOUTH PULLED into a smile again, the corners of her mouth drawn up as if tugged by the hands of an invisible plastic surgeon

She locked the front door.

"Harrison Bentley," Mom hissed. She twisted inside of herself, helpless. "Don't you get it? Take out that electric book, screen-thing of yours and see who he was."

Fin retrieved the laptop from her bag and tapped away at the keyboard. Within seconds, the internet brought up the desired results.

- *Hollywood Manager Whereabouts Unknown After Starlet Disappearance*

- *Did Bentley and Lyons Run Away Together?*

- *No Leads in Strange Hollywood Cold Case*

- *Hollywood Mystery: Actress and Manager Gone*

She scrolled further down and clicked on another headline. It led to a blog which featured a collection of notable and obscure Hollywood scandals, broken down by decade and year. Accompanying the article was a candid shot of Meredith with a younger version of the man who'd just fled. They had been spied leaving a restaurant. It was another photo outside Musso & Frank, a sister shot to the one she'd seen in *Whispers*. Fin recalled the entry from Mom's diary that mentioned the intrusive paparazzi. Bentley faced the camera in an adversarial way. One arm was stretched toward the camera in a defensive gesture, the other wrapped around her mother. Meredith was looking straight ahead, her face unreadable. They didn't look like they were having a good time.

Could this really be the same guy as the old man next door? Everything is so fucking insane that it's hard to believe... But there's no reason the ghost inside me would lie. And the truth feels like a boulder in my stomach.

Scrolling further down, a gossip story that wasn't in her binder of clippings appeared. Someone had scanned the article. She hadn't seen this one until now, though before this week, she hadn't searched for anything on her mother in some time. The date of the blog post told her that it had been written just last year. The newspaper print was old but still readable when she zoomed in on it:

May 7, 1980, Hollywood, CA—A year has passed since the strange disappearance of rising actress Meredith Lyons, and the case has seemingly been closed. The world moves fast in this industry, and with no leads, the police have come up empty-handed. Lyons's apartment did not show signs of a break-in. Her ex-husband, actor Theodore Slattery, did not notice much missing when called to search through the belongings in her apartment.

The only missing items of note were one suitcase and Lyons's trademark garnet ring. This leads authorities to believe that Lyons simply up and left, but that does not explain why she abandoned the two-year-old child she and Slattery had together, Finley.

Furthermore, Running to the Sea *had yet to wrap. Although Lyons had finished shooting all of her scenes, she was obligated to remain local in case she was needed for additional scenes or script changes as requested by the studio. Lyons was also expected to be available after principal photography had finished, in case of pick-ups. For those not in the know, this is a term sometimes known as "re-shoots," a common practice to capture more footage after a film has been edited. This can happen if it's decided that the film needs additional story elements or "sprucing up," intended to hone the story to its desired form.*

Several sources that have requested to be off the record described Lyons as free-spirited but professional in her work life, willing to fulfill any and all obligations to the production and studio, and unlikely to breach contract. These same sources have admitted that they feared for Lyons's safety on occasion. Slattery was witnessed in disarray and screaming at Lyons in public on more than one occasion. From what this publication can gather, the two were last seen together in the parking lot of Musso & Frank, a Hollywood restaurant popular with heavy-hitting, studio decision-makers, and seasoned and up-and-coming stars.

Less reported on is the fact that Lyons's manager Harrison Bentley has also disappeared, sometime after Lyons. Those who knew them have guessed that they'd become intimately involved after working together, and sources close to the actress speculate that Bentley was the cause of Lyons's break with Slattery.

It has also been suggested that former actor Bentley was becoming ferocious in his growing jealousy of Lyons's success, as well as her growing friendships with male co-stars and others in her orbit, such as studio vice presidents and various agents courting her business.

Bentley was initially questioned as a person of interest, but evidence only amounted to hearsay. He was reportedly "nervous, sweaty, and bereft," according to those who saw him in the weeks following Lyons's disappearance. This was right before he himself went missing. Estimates place Bentley's own absence around six to eight weeks later.

Lyons's closest co-star in Running to the Sea, *British actor Roy Treadwell, was rumored to have been seeing Lyons as well. They were good friends, and were occasionally seen getting very cozy together, both on set and off. Treadwell has been questioned and cleared. Everyone who worked on the production has also been cleared of wrongdoing, this publication has heard. Treadwell and the rest of the cast and crew had still been filming during the week of Lyons's disappearance. Additionally, the hours were long, which kept everyone busy. The production reportedly shot for fourteen to sixteen hours each day.*

In any case, it is nigh unthinkable for an actor or actress to skip the biggest night of the year in their profession without good reason. The 52nd Academy Awards took place only last month at the Dorothy Chandler Pavilion in Los Angeles. Most of the above-the-line crew on the film attended, including Treadwell, who won and accepted his Oscar for Best Supporting Actor. While onstage, he mentioned his missing co-star in a heartfelt tribute.

Anyone with helpful information should contact the Los Angeles Police Department. You can also contact us here at the Golden Scoop.

And that was the end of the article. It may have been the last thing written about Mom, this guesswork on an actress that had become a footnote in the great compendium of Hollywood scandals.

A sense of finality hit Fin. She closed the laptop and laid her head in her hands, grief blanketing her. Tears spilled down her face.

"Charlie isn't Charlie," Mom said.

"I know," Fin said. "But I don't feel well, and I don't think I can do this anymore."

"Sleep," Mom replied. "There's more to come."

WHEN FIN WOKE, she felt more like herself. She stretched and looked around, recalling the bizarre and worrying events of the day. *Was I out for an hour? Two?* The light in the sky didn't seem much different from when she passed out.

Her computer. She sat up, grabbed the thing like it burned, and shoved it back in her bag along with all the other Meredith obsessions.

Perhaps it was time to cut this getaway short. She didn't know if this… *possession* would follow her home, but she hoped at least the weirdo phone calls would stop. *Couldn't hurt to leave and see what happens, I guess.*

A spiral formed in the air a few feet away. It looked like a puddle rippling, and it spun slowly. *What the fuck now?*

Soft light broke through from the middle of the aberration, stretching itself toward her.

And then her phone rang.

"Unknown" splayed across the caller ID. She answered the call.

"Yes?" she whispered.

CLICK, CLICK, POP, CLICK.

"There's no time left, Mom," the voice on the other end said.

Mom?

"Tilt left, not right. You won't go over the cliff." Then the connection dropped.

Who else but Marnie would refer to Fin as Mom? But the voice didn't sound like Marnie; it barely sounded human.

I'll MAKE it stop. I'm leaving. Now.

The air around Fin cradled her like it wanted to keep her there. The light in the portal faded, and the anomaly slowed its spinning. It rippled inward and blinked out of sight.

She'd have to figure out this craziness later. *And if I never do, that's fine too!* She pocketed the phone, rose, and walked to the bedroom on legs laden with purpose. Moving still felt like walking under water, however, so she called on every iota of strength she possessed.

Fin whipped out her suitcase from the closet, tossed it onto the bed, and turned back to the closet to rip her clothes from the hangers. Fin grabbed a second armload when—

Green light spilled onto the closet floor. It appeared to be coming from a crack at the base of the wall. There was a tiny bit of space between the floor and drywall there, where a seal should have been. *How did I not notice this before?*

Fin pushed a group of hangers aside to find another crack, which stretched from ceiling to floor. Her pulse skyrocketed. She needed to leave this place immediately. But against her will, her hand reached out to the wall, felt for a particular spot, and pushed. A hidden spring mechanism clicked, and the wall swung slowly open.

Behind the secret door was a small room. A dusty lump of sheets were on the floor.

I should run. Finish packing and get in the car and never fucking come back here. Or better yet, just leave everything and GO.

But Fin was not in control of herself. More-so, she had to know what this was. There was no reason to stow an ordinary household staple in such a manner, unless it was important to hide it from the outside world. She kneeled down, gripped the cotton bundle in her fingers, and dragged it toward her.

In the depths of the faded fabric, she found fur. Multiple shades of white, brown, orange, and black, all sewn together. Fin ran her hand over the velvety treasure, and unraveled the sheet that protected it. Wrapped inside, she found a small, multicolored fur jacket which had seen better days. Some of the leather trim had deteriorated, and portions of the fur had nearly separated from the whole, dangling in soft clumps.

The familiar lasso feeling again. She was at the mercy of her ghost puppeteer once more.

"See," Meredith hissed.

Fin felt herself put the jacket on.

Then her pupils faded away, and her eyes turned all white.

But she saw.

THEO SAT ON a park bench with an old-school briefcase at his side. He was decades younger, impatient, and wearing sunglasses.

Another man around the same age sat down on the other end of the bench. He also wore sunglasses. Something about him seemed off. This man was fidgety. Beads of sweat collected on his forehead and rolled down his face from under the Ray-Bans. "Theo," he breathed. "It's done. I—"

"Don't use my name," Theo snapped. He sat up straighter and surveyed the area. He was colder and much calmer than the other guy. "And I don't want to know anything else but this: Is she wrapped?"

His companion took off his shades and wiped his face with his shirt sleeve. Fin recognized him now. This was Harrison, now known as *Charlie*. His face was indeed a little different, as if he'd had work done, but it was definitely the same man. Harrison grew sullen, as if just now realizing he had committed a heinous and irreversible act.

Theo repeated himself, now glaring at Harrison from over the top of his sunglasses. "Is she wrapped?"

Harrison nodded.

Theo shoved the briefcase at Harrison, who fumbled but caught it. He clicked the case open and peaked inside. Stacks upon stacks of cash, as promised. He clacked the case shut, eyes darting around.

"Thank you for your help on the production," Theo said. "However, this will be your last. I better not see your face in this town again."

"What?" This had come as a surprise to Harrison.

"You heard me." Theo snatched Harrison by his collar with both fists. The briefcase fell to the ground. "I don't care where you go or what you do, but I suggest you leave this state. Change your name, your face, burn your fingerprints off—I don't care." Theo gave him a shake. "Because you're responsible for this—ALL of it. If I see you again, you sniveling little shit, I'll be handing a pile of money to the next guy. Understand?" Another shake, rougher this time. *Again! This time with feeling!*

Terror infused every ragged breath Harrison took. He could only swallow and nod.

Theo shoved Harrison off the bench and stood. He loomed over the man and made an abrupt move as if he were going to attack (*just like Jeff*), a final threat before stalking away.

And... Cut!

FIN MOANED. *THE weight of such knowledge is unbearable.* But like everything else terrible she'd experienced, she'd had no say in the matter. She tried blinking her eyes back into the usual position so she could see, but they wouldn't obey.

"Now you know," Meredith said.

Fin groaned and twisted as her limbs dragged on the floor. "No...more..." she gasped, fighting for her own voice.

"Almost done," her mother promised.

CREAM-COLORED CARPET SOAKING up a puddle of red. *No, no, no, no, not this again—*

Her vision widened, zooming out to reveal the full picture. Jeff's face appeared, his head on the rug, feeding the stain with his blood. His eyes were vacant, his body lifeless.

From a distance, Fin saw herself standing over him with a heavy, cast iron pan in her hand.

Her eyes were rolled back and white.

FIN SCREAMED. "I didn't do it! I didn't do that!!" She backed herself against a wall. Her eyes worked again! She was in the hidden space within the closet and wearing her mother's rabbit jacket.

Fin's eyes rolled white again, and her lips smiled. "You're right," Mom agreed. She stroked the fur on Fin's arms as if soothing a worried pet.

Fin could hear her mother's thoughts. The connected rabbit pelts were familiar. The fur jacket was a gift from Roy. Roy was her home. Her future had been brutally torn from her.

"You didn't do this. I used you to get rid of him, like they got rid of me. They'll never find him," Mom murmured.

Groaning, Fin twisted. She let out a strangled shriek. *This is worse than Hell! I'm trapped in some kind of fucked up, purgatorial loop.* Were they destined to play out these events again and again until they somehow got things right? No matter, the authorities would find evidence that would lead to Jeff's body. No one would ever believe that her dead, missing actress mother possessed her and killed him, then got rid of all traces of the event.

"You're sick," Fin gasped, tears flowing.

"I'm a lot of things," Mom answered. "Harlot, actress, puppet, whore, difficult... *Mrs. Don't.* I didn't mean to scare Marnie, by the way. I was just trying to warn her. You have a future now. I did it for you and Marnie. But I needed this too."

Fin felt her own hand stroking her face and hair.

"For love. For vengeance," Mom explained.

"No more," Fin pleaded.

CREAK.

Fin regained control of her sight just in time to see a pair of feet on the floor in front of her. The feet led to legs, and the legs led—all the way up—to Harrison Bentley.

He held a baseball bat against his shoulder.

"I know who you are," he said. "And I'm sorry I have to do this."

And then he swung.

FLASHES OF SKY. The feeling of being dragged against gravel, then dirt.

Again? Think. Breathe. What can I feel?

Throbbing pain.

Didn't this happen already? Am I in a time loop?

Harrison was towing her on the sled again. But this time they were headed into the woods, not out of them. She squinted against the sunlight. The cliff overlooking the sea was getting closer.

He's pulling me towards the edge. Oh-my-God, oh-my-God, oh-my-God, Marnie. I have to get home to Marnie!

"No," Fin moaned.

Harrison looked back at her, furtive. "Shit," he hissed.

The edge of the cliff was coming up too fast. *No-no-no-no-no—*

"Sorry, kid," Harrison muttered. "You weren't supposed to find that jacket. None of this was supposed to happen. But I can't just let you go."

The cold Pacific grew louder, crashing against the rocks below. Fin's heart rate sped up. She began to hyperventilate.

"You understand that right? Theo would kill me if he knew you found out. I need to protect myself." The bat he'd slugged her with was tucked away in the back of his jacket like a sword.

I have to get home. I have to get home to Marnie.

The world spun around her. Fin clutched her head and struggled to sit up. The sled was at the edge now.

Harrison blinked away tears. "I really am sorry. I loved your mother." He looked as terrorized as Fin felt. "I don't know why any of this is happening, but it's almost over. You'll be in a better place soon. Say hello to Meredith for me, will you? I miss her." He unsheathed his bat.

"You FUCK!" Meredith spat.

Harrison's eyes went wide, and his grip on the bat nearly loosened.

Fin closed her eyes and saw a terrible vision of her mother. It was 1979 again, and her body was limp in Harrison's arms. Same woods, same cliff. He tossed her body over the side without much thought or effort. Mom disappeared into the cold sea below.

Harrison readied his weapon.

Fin recalled the voice from the phone call.

"Tilt left, not right."

Harrison swung.

Against her instinct, Fin threw herself left, toward Harrison and toward the blow, rather than to the right, which would have resulted in her falling over the cliff's edge.

The bat whooshed over her head, and she slammed shoulder-first into the dirt. She then lifted both legs and barreled her feet hard into the back of Harrison's knees. He collapsed forward, and she kicked him again.

This time, he was the one that went over the edge.

Fin crawled to the edge and leaned over, watched Harrison's body splash into the water below. She watched for several minutes, until she was certain he wasn't coming back up.

She spit over the side in his honor.

MALIBU

SATURDAY

SUNNY LOS ANGELES. Home, though not for long. A good day as any to die.

Theo Slattery sat in his wheelchair, wearing linen and a pair of shades. There in his backyard, he watched the waves of the Pacific. It was a breathtaking view, the kind that only the rich can afford.

From nearby bushes, Fin watched him. The house manager had recognized her and let her in, trusting her to see herself out back. She considered wheeling Theo to the perimeter of his property, and with a simple tilt, send his frail body sailing from the wheelchair into the cold surf below—maybe his bones would snap in two dozen pieces on those big, sharp rocks—but the possibility that Theo's house manager, or another servant, would catch her was too big of a risk.

This was the first time in years Fin had seen her father in person, and it would also be the last.

The morning was brisk, so she'd worn Mom's fur jacket. First she drove Marnie to school like any other parent, but then she kept driving all the way to the coast.

"Why don't we go visit Dad?" she had asked the empty car. "I think it's time for a family reunion."

She felt a dark, gleeful agreement inside her.

Fin straightened. She no longer cared if Theo saw or heard her. She called for assistance, using Meredith's words. "For love. For vengeance." She then felt her mother put Fin on the same way she would the fur jacket. Fin's eyes then went white, and a huge grin spread across her face. She knew she looked insane. And man, had she felt it too.

Fuck it. What a finale.

This was the only way Mom would leave, Fin had learned. Fin would get her life back only after this final loose end was tied.

Old Theo didn't look half as powerful as he once did in the past, like in that horrible scene when he'd thrown a briefcase full of money at Harrison. "It's been a long time," he said.

"It certainly has," Meredith Lyons agreed.

Theo paled at the sound. A shaking hand dotted with age spots pulled the shades from his face. It was the haunted face of a man who had just seen a ghost. "Meredith?" he croaked.

A corner of Fin's mouth pulled up, cold. "Hello."

Theo sucked in a desperate wheeze of air and grasped at his chest. He thrashed in his chair, growing weaker.

"I'll see you in Hell," Fin said. She bared her teeth under the brim of her fabulous '70s-style sunglasses.

The impossible sneer of his murdered ex-wife was the last thing Theo Slattery saw before the lights went out. His shell fell back into the wheelchair, his last breath whistling out of him.

Fin felt something leave her. She felt lighter, almost buoyant. She inhaled deeply, as if this was the very first breath of her life, and smiled. Fin began to walk away from the scene, but something nagged at her.

Let someone else find the fucker and deal with his corpse.

When she got back to her car, she saw two voicemails waiting on her phone. One was from her *Unknown* caller, and the other was from a foreign number. She put the cell to her ear and listened to the first message.

The familiar *click, click, pop, click.*

"You did it," the voice said. It glitched and morphed, layering over itself, until it became clear enough to recognize. "It's going to be okay now," Marnie said. The message ended.

The second recording was warm and seasoned. British. Formal. "Hello, Fin. This is Roy Treadwell. Thank you so much for getting in touch. I hope this message finds you well. Apologies for the delay; I've only just gotten your email relayed from my agency. Merry—your mother— was a dear friend. Far more, if I'm being honest. I—" His voice cracked. There was dead air then, and Fin wondered if he'd hung up after reassessing the message. But a shuddering intake of breath from the other side of the world told her otherwise. "I'd love to catch up with you if you're amenable. Please call back when you can. I sincerely look forward to speaking with you." *Click.*

She listened to Roy's recording again. His voice did something to her. He sounded kind. He sounded concerned. He *cared.*

Tears streaked down Fin's face as she hugged the phone to her chest, body wracking with quiet sobs.

It seemed that Fin and Marnie had a future after all.

ACKNOWLEDGMENTS

FIRST OFF, THANK you to the love of all of my lives, my other half, Steve. I simply could not have written this book without your love, kindness, and support. Same goes for embarking on my first feature film, *House of Ashes,* which happened to coincide with writing my first novella. It's been absolute madness. I have walked through enough fire that I have become it, and it's because I've had you by my side.

To my family: thank you! And I promise that none of this is about you. Well, except maybe that one guy.

Another massive thank you goes to Sadie "Mother Horror" Hartmann, who was enthusiastic and open to even reading my spec manuscript in the first place, for her imprint under Dark Matter Ink, Dark Hart Books. I adore you, and I'm so proud to know you, Sadie. You do so much for indie genre publishing, a total rock star. She not only wanted *I Can See Your Lies* (my first-ever book!), but she also wanted to know all about the genre-filmmaker-written *Haunted Reels* anthology put together by my kick-ass producer-friend and brother-from-another-mother, David Lawson, Jr., aka Smiling Dave. I'm in that first anthology, and it's filled with amazing genre-film friends. I love you, Dave!

And for that matter, thank you to my publisher, Rob Carroll, for going for both projects! It's been a crazy year filled with little time and too many things to do, and I appreciate you coming along for these wild rides.

A very special thank you goes to my dear friend Christopher Golden, one of my biggest supporters. Even though I've written for most of my existence, I never truly believed I could get anything seriously published until I snatched a crumb of courage from the ether and sent the first short story of my modern life to him. He replied on a thread of other wonderful New England horror and thriller authors with: "So, Izzy can write!" I don't know if you recall that kindness way back in…maybe 2014, Chris, but I do. You're one of the great ones, not just because of your talent, but because of your deep humanity and kindness. You're one of the few that sends the elevator back down, and I adore you. Thank you for being my forever-friend.

To Olly Jeavons, my fantastic cover artist, your talent is immense, and I couldn't be happier with how my baby book has gone out into the world. I've gone through much heartache writing her, but you've dressed her up in such an incredible cloak that says, "Hey world, I'm here, and I'm raw and brimming with intensity, but I'm ready as I'll ever be, and I'm fucking beautiful." I'll always be grateful for such a jaw-dropping cover, Olly.

To author and developmental editor, C. S. Humble, for not only the insightful edits, but for writing the most inspiring pep talks I've ever received. You do not seem like you're from this era, Seth. It's as if you've been transported here to bless us with your insane talent and insights.

Thank you and apologies to Grady Hendrix for his *Mr. Don't* inspiring my *Mrs. Don't*—in name only, ha-ha. Thank you to Brea Grant, not just for the blurb, but for being a friend and champion, and for your undying support. I love you and want all the joy in the world to be yours. A deep-hearted thank you to my absolute rockstar film brothers, Cargill and Aaron Moorhead, for showing me such kindness and support, a rarity in this business. You, sirs, are a dying breed, and I am honored to know you. I love you both, always.

To Karmen Wells for being a force of nature. You're wonderful, and I hope everything you dream of happens for you. To Ryan Lewis, Philip Fracassi, and Brian McAuley, for the great advice on this journey. Thank you to all of the authors and filmmakers who read my book for a blurb. I know that doing so for a first-time author is a huge leap of faith, and I deeply appreciate the trust you had in me. Speaking of which, a big ol' thanks to my beta readers, some of whom are also blurbers: Steve Johanson, Tim Meyer, Jerry Sampson, Maude Michaud, James Sabata, and Karmen again (rockstar).

To you reading this right now: THANK YOU. I hope your journey with Fin was one you won't soon forget. Last, and very much not least, dear reader, if you've ever been othered or made to feel lesser than for existing in any way, this book is especially for you. I hope you heal and that you've felt empowerment in some way within these pages.

Until next time, keep dreaming, my friends.

—Izzy Lee
Los Angeles
January 2024

ABOUT THE AUTHOR

PROFILED IN *CHRONICLE* and named as one of *A.V. Club*'s "10 female filmmakers to hire," Izzy Lee is a director on the rise. Lee has directed more than two dozen shorts, and shadowed director Adam Egypt Mortimer on the SpectreVision film *Archenemy*. She's currently in post on a long-awaited feature film. Several of her short stories have found publication, including "The Beginning" in Dark Matter INK's *Haunted Reels* anthology, curated by David Lawson, Jr.

Lee's award-winning tales have screened at major international genre festivals, such as Fantasia, Overlook, Morbido, FrightFest, Fantaspoa, Brooklyn Horror, Boston Sci-Fi, Boston Underground, Chattanooga, and more. From 2022-2023, Lee earned five Certificates of Completion from Sundance Collab's directing, producing, and visual storytelling courses.

I Can See Your Lies is her first book.

Also Available or Coming Soon from Dark Matter INK

Human Monsters: A Horror Anthology
Edited by Sadie Hartmann & Ashley Saywers
ISBN 978-1-958598-00-9

Zero Dark Thirty: The 30 Darkest Stories from Dark Matter Magazine, 2021–'22 Edited by Rob Carroll
ISBN 978-1-958598-16-0

Linghun by Ai Jiang
ISBN 978-1-958598-02-3

Monstrous Futures: A Sci-Fi Horror Anthology
Edited by Alex Woodroe
ISBN 978-1-958598-07-8

Our Love Will Devour Us by R. L. Meza
ISBN 978-1-958598-17-7

Haunted Reels: Stories from the Minds of Professional Filmmakers Curated by David Lawson
ISBN 978-1-958598-13-9

The Vein by Steph Nelson
ISBN 978-1-958598-15-3

Other Minds by Eliane Boey
ISBN 978-1-958598-19-1

Monster Lairs: A Dark Fantasy Horror Anthology
Edited by Anna Madden
ISBN 978-1-958598-08-5

Frost Bite by Angela Sylvaine
ISBN 978-1-958598-03-0

The Bleed by Stephen S. Schreffler
ISBN 978-1-958598-11-5

Free Burn by Drew Huff
ISBN 978-1-958598-26-9

The House at the End of Lacelean Street
by Catherine McCarthy
ISBN 978-1-958598-23-8

The Dead Spot: Stories of Lost Girls
by Angela Sylvaine
ISBN 978-1-958598-27-6

Chopping Spree by Angela Sylvaine
ISBN 978-1-958598-31-3

When the Gods Are Away by Robert E. Harpold
ISBN 978-1-958598-47-4

Grim Root by Bonnie Jo Stufflebeam
ISBN 978-1-958598-36-8

Voracious by Belicia Rhea
ISBN 978-1-958598-25-2

Abducted by Patrick Barb
ISBN 978-1-958598-37-5

Darkly Through the Glass Place by Kirk Bueckert
ISBN 978-1-958598-48-1

Beautiful Ways We Break Each Other Open
by Angela Liu
ISBN 978-1-958598-60-3

The Off-Season: An Anthology of Coastal New Weird
Edited by Marissa van Uden
ISBN 978-1-958598-24-5

The Exodontists by Drew Huff
ISBN 978-1-958598-64-1

The Threshing Floor by Steph Nelson
ISBN 978-1-958598-49-8

Club Contango by Eliane Boey
ISBN 978-1-958598-57-3

Psychopomp by Maria Dong
ISBN 978-1-958598-52-8

Little Red Flags: An Anthology of Control and Deceit
Edited by Noelle W. Ihli & Steph Nelson
ISBN 978-1-958598-54-2

The Divine Flesh by Drew Huff
ISBN 978-1-958598-59-7

Frost Bite 2 by Angela Sylvaine
ISBN 978-1-958598-55-9

Part of the Dark Hart Collection

Rootwork by Tracy Cross
ISBN 978-1-958598-01-6

Mosaic by Catherine McCarthy
ISBN 978-1-958598-06-1

Apparitions by Adam Pottle
ISBN 978-1-958598-18-4

A Gathering of Weapons by Tracy Cross
ISBN 978-1-958598-38-2

Printed in the USA
CPSIA information can be obtained
at www.ICGtesting.com
LVHW090927070524
779566LV00003B/488